Crushed

Crushed

JENNIFER
K. THOMAS

ISBN 978-1-7323987-0-2 (Print)
ISBN 978-1-7323987-1-9 (ePub)
ISBN 978-1-7323987-2-6 (Kindle)

Library of Congress Control Number 2018946125

Cover design by Fiona Jayde/Fiona Jayde Media
Interior formatting by Tamara Cribley/The Deliberate Page
Edited by Indie Solutions

Printed in the United States of America.
Published by On The Verge Publishing
P.O. Box 891633, Temecula, CA 92589
Visit www.authorjenniferkthomas.com

To Kathi

Without your encouragement, my stories may have remained trapped in my head forever.

Thank you for all your advice and your enthusiastic support of my identity crisis.

Chapter 1

I used to think whoever said "there is a thin line between love and hate" was a complete moron. I didn't understand it. I love my family and friends with my whole being. I couldn't imagine ever hating any one of them. Sure, I could be angry with or even disappointed in them. But hate? That simply wasn't a word I would ever use, let alone feel. Turns out I am the moron.

Yesterday I loved my husband.

We sat across from each other last night at the dinner table. We recounted our days at work over spaghetti and garlic bread. We laughed and sipped wine as our daughter told us a joke her teacher had told the class. We all talked excitedly about our upcoming vacation to Orlando this summer. He went to bed early, almost right after dinner. He'd had a long day and was tired. I didn't think anything more of it.

I crawled into our bed and read for an hour or so before falling asleep. My only worries were those concerning the normal stuff: what I needed to accomplish at work, trying to remember if I signed the field trip permission slip that was due at school, and whether I had requested the day off for that trip. I fell asleep without any gratitude for how uncomplicated my life was. That was yesterday.

Today I hate him.

I hate that I believed he was different, that I believed he would stay. I hate that I was stupid enough to trust and marry someone who could laugh with me and lie to me in the same conversation. I hate that I married someone who could sleep soundly next to me at night, without any trace of remorse or guilt. I hate him for ruining our family.

The shock of reading the texts this morning, the ones I was never meant to see, was overwhelming. I had grabbed Amelia's tablet off the floor so that it didn't get stepped on. The tablet, the one he bought for her birthday even though I said she was too young to need it, displayed an unread notification on the messaging app. I opened it, wanting to make sure my seven-year-old hadn't accidentally stumbled onto something she shouldn't. I quickly realized the tablet was somehow linked to and mirroring his phone.

The unexpectedness of it left me confused and numb at first. That numbness encapsulated me long enough to get Amelia to school without drawing too much suspicion. I was quieter than normal, but that's not something a child would necessarily notice. Even if she did, she didn't ask me anything about it. By the time I dropped her off, called in sick to work, and made it back home, Grant had left for work.

I've been sitting on the couch for the past hour, silent and unmoving. What did I do wrong? Had I missed something? Was I blind to some character flaw I should have seen? Were there warning signs? Could I have stopped this devastation, or had it been inevitable?

I don't have the answers to these questions right now, but I will have plenty of time to figure them out. I'm going to have plenty of time for lots of things because I'm going to be alone. For the first time since I saw the texts this morning, I cry. Not a normal, that-was-a-sad-movie cry, but a gasping-for-air meltdown. The sounds I'm making and the contortions I can imagine splayed across my face fill me with a rush of embarrassment. I feel like I'm decomposing from the inside out. I don't know how much pain, how much torture, the human body can withstand. At some point it must simply give up, seeking rest. I must be near that breaking point.

I allow myself to experience all of it. Time moves in slow motion, and I feel like I've spent years on this couch. Gradually, something flips in my brain. It's not that the pain goes away, but my resolve to overcome has been growing. When it grows larger than the hurt and fear, I get up. I pack bags through my sobs instead of being paralyzed by them. I pack my stuff and Amelia's. I know I'll never keep her from him, but she is coming with me.

My crying intensifies when I think about my daughter, my sweet little girl, who has no clue that her life changed in an instant. My father left when I was old enough to understand dads aren't supposed to pick up and move across the country with their new family. They aren't supposed to forget they once had another life, another child. I regret my decision to leave will hurt her, but I can't remain here and pretend either. I contemplate staying. Part of me wishes I could, for her sake, but I'm just not built that way. I push through my grief and doubt.

Outsiders would say we have a perfect life. Yesterday, I would have said we had a good one. My time with Grant began as a series of moments. Glances that led to conversations. Conversations that led to a relationship. A relationship that led to a family. It ended abruptly, at least for me. It ended with me finding those damn texts this morning.

For the first time, I have no plan. This thought stops me in my tracks and causes the room to spin. I push through and load my car anyway. I don't know what my new life will look like, but I have no choice but to continue moving forward. I decide to do one more thing before I leave our family home.

Four months after leaving Grant, I'm still searching for normalcy. My feelings change daily, sometimes hourly. Some days I convince myself I made the best decision in leaving that day. I tell myself that leaving will be viewed as courageous someday. Other days I miss Grant terribly and force myself not to dial his number. Most days I'm simply sad. I distract myself by making Amelia my primary focus, making sure she is adjusting. My career has been especially challenging and a welcome distraction. The weekends I don't have Amelia with me are the hardest. I stay in pajamas, eat ice cream, and read self-help books well into the early morning hours. My mother and friends love me enough to realize my moping and sadness have gone on long enough, past the point of being helpful or healthy. Over the past several weeks, they have encouraged (or demanded) I start to act more like the strong woman they know I am. I feel more like a wounded bird, wanting to take flight but not having the strength to make it happen yet.

The first few times I was dragged out of my house, in makeup I didn't want to wear and heels I wished were slippers, were painful. Lucky for me, my mother and girlfriends are a tenacious bunch. I act as though I resent their persistence. They grow more determined.

A couple weekends ago, I found myself suggesting a new restaurant I wanted to try. There was a look of victory in my mother's eyes, but she simply said, "Sounds good."

My risotto dinner was excellent, and I enjoyed joking with my mother about my crazy aunt who lives in Florida. She's not actually crazy, but she's into new age stuff, like crystals and aura readings. I made one mistake during dinner though. I mentioned my ten-year high school reunion was coming up. My mother was relentless. She went on and on about me needing to get out and have fun. I told her I'd rather go to the dentist. She frowned and said I had to have a better attitude if I wanted to be happy again. I do want to be happy, so after several more rounds of "will she or won't she go to her reunion," I caved and agreed to make an appearance.

That is why I find myself walking from the valet toward a high-rise hotel in downtown San Diego this evening instead of being in my favorite pair of yoga pants, enjoying a pint of cookies and cream. Reunions are awkward under the best of circumstances. I do not consider going through a divorce an ideal conversation starter. My plan is to try to avoid the topic as much as possible.

My senses are assaulted when I walk into the ballroom. Loud music from my youth is blasting through the DJ's speakers as colorful lights swirl across the walls and ceiling. Mixed with the hip-hop song currently being pumped through the room are the sounds of muted conversation and polite laughter. I see dozens of semi-familiar faces. I haven't seen or even talked to most of these people in years. With the advent of social media, many people choose to keep in touch with old high school friends, but I haven't had the same desire.

I head to the bar to grab a drink and order a glass of red wine without thinking. I take one sip and realize it's too sweet for my liking. I order a dirty martini instead.

I sip my drink and watch the room. Women in cocktail dresses, ones they bought especially for tonight, flitter around, squealing in delight at seeing old friends. They ask each other about marriages and families and where they found their fabulous dresses. Men in suits, the same ones they wear to any other occasion requiring them to dress up, engage in more serious conversations. My guess is they are discussing their careers and trying to convey as much success as their bland attire and uninteresting positions will permit. Going to a party as an adult isn't much different than going as a teenager. You scan the room hoping to find someone you know to talk to, someone you want to talk to.

I nervously twirl one of my dark brown curls, notice, and force myself to stop. This is where keeping in touch with some people would have been helpful. I actually enjoyed high school for the most part and had some good friends, but I left it all behind. Reminiscing about that time of my life stirs up some heartfelt emotions and some painful memories for me. Avoiding these feelings has been a great coping mechanism for me up until this point. Being here, surrounded by music I listened to after school while I lay on my bed doing homework, and by colorful balloons in our school colors of blue, white, and silver, I can no longer hide from the memories.

I met Luke my freshman year at Rancho Bernardo High School. We'd gone to different middle schools, so our paths hadn't crossed before. He was a sophomore and already had a reputation for being one of the best baseball players at the school. He was athletic, smart, and fearless. Some guys are confident to the point of being cocky, but not Luke. He had enough confidence to make him stand out, but not so much that he alienated anyone. Despite his popularity, he didn't have a girlfriend at Rancho Bernardo. He'd gone on a few dates, but never anything more than that.

I was getting lunch one day with my friend Karen when I saw him with my neighbor, Matt. Matt and I used to play together when we were younger, but once boy/girl segregation became socially important in elementary school, we went our separate ways. Our friendship never recovered, and we moved on to different social groups. I noticed Matt and Luke looking in our direction and talking. I looked away when they caught me staring at them and didn't dare a glance back in their direction. I was caught off guard when they walked over to us. I don't know if I was nervous because I hadn't talked to Matt in years or because Luke was with him, but I started to overheat. I wasn't necessarily shy, but when caught off guard I could get flustered. I made it a point not to make eye contact with Luke, since I was sure it was Matt who was coming over to talk to me.

"Hey Jess." Matt was acting as if we talked all the time.

"Hey Matt, what's up?" I answered, trying to sound cooler than I felt.

"Nothing much. What did you get for lunch?"

"Um, pizza."

"Cool," he replied. He paused before adding, "This is my friend, Luke. Luke, this is Jessica."

7

I finally allowed myself to take Luke in. I had never seen him this close. My teenage hormones seemed to be doing laps through my body, causing my heart to race and my stomach to flutter. He was beautiful. It made me uncomfortable to look at him directly. His bright blue eyes made me feel too vulnerable when I gazed into them. "Hi." It was all I could say before I had to turn away.

"Aren't you in my geometry class?"

I glanced at him again. He was smiling at me. "Yeah, I think so."

"That class is killer. Are you good at math?"

"I guess so." I shrugged and took a deep breath. My heartbeat began to slow. He wanted help with his math. Any number of people could have told him I was good at it and would make a good study partner choice. It suddenly made sense why they were talking to me.

"Maybe you can help me sometime? I need to get my grade up in that class before Coach finds out I'm not doing so great." He flashed me the most dazzling smile I'd ever seen. I forgot to breathe for several seconds. I remember wondering if he knew how disarming that smile was or if he just threw it around, unaware of its power.

I'm pretty sure if he used that smile on Mrs. Mendoza, our geometry teacher, even she would have helped him. "Sure, I can do that." I wasn't surprised, but it was a letdown to discover he was only interested in my brain. I watched his fingers quickly type my number into his phone so we could set up a study time.

Our food was ready, and it was time for us to return to our tables of friends. "Sounds like I'll be talking to you again soon, Jessica. Thanks." Luke flashed another smile at me.

"No, thank *you*." I immediately wished I had only nodded, or waved or had a seizure.

The boys had longer strides than us and ended up walking in front of us.

Karen grabbed my arm and leaned in to whisper. "That was awesome. He's so hot."

I smiled back at her, feeling my cheeks flush. Karen and I began to giggle.

Luke glanced back at us over his shoulder. "Hey, quit checking me out!" He winked and turned away before I had a chance to respond.

I never did tutor Luke in geometry, but we went on our first date that Saturday night. I got over being so awkward around him, and he admitted he'd planned the entire meeting as a way to get my number. I was flattered and excited, but also worried. I knew after that first date this boy had the power to ruin me. I also knew I wouldn't stop him.

A woman accidently nudges my elbow as she walks past me. "Sorry." She continues on without a backward glance.

"I'm sorry." My answer is automatic and unnecessary, a consequence of being overly polite.

The encounter startles me from my daydream. I sip my drink and scan the crowd until I spot someone who makes the room stand still.

He's here. I knew with the reunion being advertised as an event for several graduating classes that him being here would be a possibility. Seeing him causes instant, unwanted butterflies in my stomach. I feel like that girl in the cafeteria, so unsure and overwhelmed. It's as if all my years of maturing and growing into a confident adult have disappeared.

I'm unable to take my eyes off him as my heart throbs furiously. Luke was a good-looking kid, but he's developed into something even more impressive. His body is bigger, more muscular. His stubble makes his face appear more masculine than I remember. His light brown hair is long on top and shorter on the sides. It's perfectly disheveled and begging for hands to be run through it. His flawlessly tailored suit conveys the kind of achievement the other men in the room are faking.

As I admire the man he's become, his eyes find mine. His eyes search mine for a moment before grazing down my body. I suddenly feel warm, so I down the remainder of my martini.

I close my eyes while I do, and when I reopen them, the mood has shifted. Luke narrows his eyes slightly, and they take on a cold quality. He shakes his head before running a hand through his hair. He returns his attention to the boisterous group of men he is talking to.

I had wondered what his reaction would be, seeing me after all this time. His response causes me to feel like I've been punched in the stomach. I shouldn't be happy to see him. I have to get over whatever leftover emotions are being stirred up inside me, because it's clear from the expression on his beautiful face that this will not be a happy reunion, at least not between the two of us. If Luke can convey these sentiments from across a room, I'm afraid of what he could do with actual words. I need to stay away from him.

I'm relieved when another face I remember appears in my sight line. Matt walks toward me with a big smile on his face and a pretty brunette on his arm.

"Jessica Adams? Shit! I haven't seen you in ten years!" Matt practically yells as he embraces me in a huge bear hug.

"Hi Matt!" I can't help but match his enthusiasm. "But it's Rogers now."

"Oh, that's right." His mouth twists into a frown. It's so quick I almost miss it. "I'm glad you're here. This is my wife, Rachel."

Rachel extends her hand to me. "So nice to meet you, Jessica. I've heard so much about you."

"Nice to meet you too." I grasp her hand and wonder why she has heard about me. After Luke and I started dating, I spent most of high school hanging out with him and Matt. After we ended, so did my friendship with Matt. His family moved from the neighborhood while I was away at college, and I completely lost contact with him. Luke and Matt were very close in high school, so it's possible they are still friends. Based on the reaction I received from Luke, I doubt I'm the topic of any conversation he's been having though.

I enjoy catching up with Matt, and Rachel is lovely. The interaction gives me time to recover from Luke. I catch a glimpse of him from time to time. He's always engaged in some lively conversation and drawing the attention of women congregating nearby. He appears to be here alone though.

The night continues with lots of small talk with people I half remember. We politely ask about each other's careers, spouses, and kids. We wonder aloud what happened to those not in attendance of this awkward event. I was hoping to see Karen tonight. I owe her an apology for not keeping in touch after high school. A tall man named Chris, who I remember from my biology class, mentions she moved to Alaska with her husband about a year ago. I'm about to ask him if he knows anything else about her, but I'm interrupted when Donovan boorishly bursts into our group. I never did care much for him and his class clown antics.

The biggest success of the evening is my ability to avoid Luke. I've kept an eye on him throughout the evening, so I know he's still here. I'm thankful I haven't had to endure any more uncomfortable interactions with him, even ones across the room.

After a couple more drinks and an enjoyable conversation with Sarah, our class president, I decide this isn't as painful as I thought it may be. I let my guard down, and I'm not paying attention when a girl I know from eleventh grade drama class drags me over to a group of people to say hello. *Shit!* Standing opposite me is Luke. He stiffens and presses his lips together. I stare before I have time to think better of it. Because of his earlier reaction, I expect him to be hostile, but all I see is a flash of pain before he looks away.

The group chatters on, about what I have no idea. I can't focus on the conversation. Luke has grown unusually quiet.

"Jessica, so sorry to hear about your divorce."

The mention of my name captures my attention. A short blonde whose name I can't remember is standing next to me. She isn't wearing a wedding ring, and there is something about the way she says it that makes me wonder if we have something in common we wish we didn't. I nod and smile at her. I have no idea how news of my impending divorce has traveled so quickly. I only mentioned it to a couple of people after they specifically asked me about my marital status. Apparently, the gossip mill hasn't died down at all during the last ten years.

"I'm divorced too. Was the hardest thing I've ever been through." She places a hand on my arm.

"It's certainly not fun." I give her a small smile, wishing she would stop talking. I don't like speaking about my divorce, but I can tell she's being sincere with her empathy, so I maintain my politeness.

She leans into me. "I wore my ring for months after too."

"Oh…yeah." I avert my eyes. I don't wear my ring all the time anymore, but I thought wearing it tonight would help avoid uncomfortable questions. It seems silly and pathetic now. To make matters worse, I can feel Luke's eyes on me.

I glance at the blonde, and she offers me a nod of solidarity. She is kind enough to turn her attention to someone else. I make it a point to pay attention while she asks others about their jobs and where they are living these days. Someone addresses her by name. I regret I didn't remember her name is Rebecca before.

"Luke Taylor, handsome as ever," she says when it's Luke's turn for questions. "Wait a minute. Didn't you two used to date?" Rebecca has connected dots I wish would have stayed unconnected. I don't dare look at Luke. I don't want to see how he has reacted to the question.

"A long time ago. Excuse me," I answer and turn to walk away before Luke can say anything that would hurt or embarrass me.

Overall, I would call my reunion experience a success. I enjoyed most of it and survived being around Luke. Seeing him brought back too many feelings, good and bad. Luke is handsome and overwhelming and completely off-limits for me. Before Grant, there was Luke. Different but similar. Men who initially made me feel safe and loved. Men who both took pieces of me with them when my time with them was done.

I want those pieces back.

Chapter 2

The next couple weeks at work are busy. We're completing a quarter end, and as the controller, I have increased responsibilities to manage beyond my regular duties. In addition to completing financials, the management team is still searching for investors for the winery where I work. The market in Temecula continues to grow, and we want to be able to compete well into the future. The good thing about me being overloaded at work is that it makes it difficult for me to find time to overanalyze the reunion and my interactions with Luke.

I'm exhausted by the time the weekend arrives. Grant was supposed to help Amelia with her school project last weekend, but he made up some lame excuse about not having enough time. We've only been separated for a few months, but I can already tell he's going to be a Disneyland Dad. He picks Amelia up every other Friday from school, takes her to the movies, dinner, and theme parks, and then brings her home Sunday to a boring mom who makes sure her homework is done and that she eats her vegetables. It makes me angry, but mainly sad. I worry our relationship will be affected because I don't get to be the fun parent anymore. Cleaning the house and helping Amelia with her final report for the year will dominate the entire weekend.

The word "help" may be an understatement. She has a report about her favorite dinosaur to complete. She picked a pterodactyl. We're halfway through answering her list of questions when I realize a pterodactyl is not even really a dinosaur, but a flying reptile. I try to explain this to my daughter and convince her to change her subject. I'm potentially reading too much into the instructions for a first grade report, but I can't help it. My attention to detail is a blessing and a curse. I think about it this way: I'm either teaching Amelia a valuable lesson on the importance of fully reading directions, or I'm giving her something to discuss with her therapist in twenty years. Only time will tell.

An hour later I know more about a brachiosaur than I ever hoped to, and Amelia is whining she wants to eat dinner. I prepare a quick meal of pasta with butter and parmesan cheese. I also cook green beans. I bribe her with ice cream for dessert, so she eats them and it makes me feel like a better mom. After we finish, I help her draw a brachiosaur. She is frustrated and tired, so I draw the outline for her and she colors it in. I should have her do it, but I don't think helping her draw a dinosaur will affect her education too much. At the end of the evening I'm convinced that homework is a secret plot designed to test parenting skills. If you can survive elementary school homework, you're deemed fit and ready to tackle the teenage years.

───────────

Monday morning comes too soon. I drag myself out of my large comfortable bed. One of the benefits of sleeping alone is I can make my bed how I want. When Grant and I were first married, I made up our new king-sized bed with an extra-soft feather topper, high-thread-count white sheets, and a beautiful white down comforter. These were wedding presents from my grandmother, and I loved them. After several months, Grant informed me he couldn't sleep on the soft feather bed and the down comforter was causing him to feel too hot in the middle of the night. My beloved bedding went into the linen closet for years, until I finally sold them at a garage sale. One of the first things I did after I moved out was order the most luxurious bedding I could find.

I arrive at work a little later than usual after helping Amelia carry her large brachiosaur drawing into school. The winery is already buzzing with barbacks stocking the tasting bars and housekeepers preparing the grounds for the day's visitors. I spot Ryan, the winemaker, checking various gauges as I walk through the tank yard.

"Good morning, Ryan." I wave as I hurry toward my office.

"Morning Jess!" Ryan yells across the alley of tanks. He is sometimes flirty with me, but he's careful not to cross that line into being too pushy. We attempted to go on a date about a month ago. My one and only date since I left Grant. He took me to a local restaurant and knew how to order wines to complement the day's specials. It was a delicious meal, but it felt as romantic as dinners with my mom. After that night, I knew Ryan and I could never be more than friends, that there was something missing between us. We talked about it and both agreed.

Ryan is a good guy, the kind of guy I should want to be with. Ryan is smart and handsome, but I think his talent is his most attractive quality. Most people don't realize how science and art must be balanced to make remarkable wine. Ryan's vast understanding of the science of winemaking is impressive, but his devotion to his craft is what sets him apart as a winemaker. He loves wine and wants everyone to appreciate it the way he does. He always takes time to explain different aspects of the process to me. Sometimes the scientific terminology goes over my head, but his passion is infectious, and I enjoy hearing him talk about it. He deserves a woman who will appreciate what he has to offer. Unfortunately, as a couple we lack that extra spark.

I arrive at my office and am greeted by a big box of baked goods. I love my assistant, Linda. She's more than an assistant; she's become a friend. A friend who is keeping me from losing my breakup weight by bringing in sugary treats every Monday.

"Good morning, Linda."

"Good morning." She is already running around our little office, getting paperwork ready for the week.

"It's going to be a busy one. I need to finish up the quarterly management reports."

"You also have a meeting this afternoon with more potential investors," she reminds me.

"Right." I grab a banana muffin from the box. "How was your weekend?"

"It was good. Too short."

"Always is."

"Did you finish your dinosaur report?" She has a smile on her face. She knows from raising three kids of her own that school projects never belong only to the kids at this age.

"I did. I got all my homework done," I reply, only half kidding.

I tell her about my weekend and the pterodactyl dilemma. She says I'm overthinking it and I admit she's right. She spent the weekend visiting her oldest child in LA. She has a new story about the newest addition to her daughter's "zoo" as she calls it. Her daughter is an animal lover and has adopted several special-needs pets. I've heard so many stories over the years, and Linda tells them with such a dramatic flair that we end up laughing so hard our stomachs hurt. I've heard about a lizard with diet restrictions requiring specially prepared meals, a dog who likes to steal the cat's food, and a bird who could speak, but only said sexually explicit words. We laughed all afternoon one day guessing at who the previous owner of the bird was. The newest addition is a hairless cat who wears sweaters to stay warm. We work hard, but I like that we make our day fun too. Our office is at the back of the property in a portable unit, so our fun doesn't bother anyone.

After catching each other up on our weekends, we jump into our job responsibilities. My day is full, so I inhale my microwave pasta lunch while I continue to work. When I glance at the clock, it's already three in the afternoon.

"Your meeting is at three-thirty, Jess," Linda reminds me.

"Right. I need to take these to the tasting room." I grab the stack of reports off my desk.

"I can take them up," she offers.

"That's okay, I could use the walk," I answer, halfway out the door.

The tasting room is crowded with people enjoying wine and conversation. A young couple laughs and touches each other as they talk. They aren't wearing wedding rings, and I assume by the way they are interacting with each other that they haven't been dating long. They seem completely enamored, too fascinated with each other to be further along in their relationship. The man catches me staring at them, and I quickly look away. I feel like I was intruding on an intimate moment even though we're all standing in a crowded room.

My embarrassment turns to clumsiness, and I trip over one of the raised wooden planks of the tasting room floor. I drop the papers and catch myself on a display table nearby. I feel the blush coming to my cheeks as I bend down and hurriedly gather them. I grab the last paper and brave a glance to see who has noticed my mishap. To my relief, the patrons haven't taken any notice of my awkward display.

Relief is replaced by confusion. Familiar eyes watch me from across the room. Luke is involved in a conversation with a gentleman in a suit, but his smirk is directed at me. Every part of me freezes, except for my panicked heart. This isn't good. He's only looking at me, and it already feels like the earth has tilted.

I shift my reports to one arm and run my free hand down the side of my dress. I walk as quickly as I can, while trying to appear like I'm not hurrying, over to our cashier station. I hand the papers to our new employee. She hasn't been with the company more than a week, and I can't remember her name, but she is young and eager to prove herself.

"Good morning, Jessica. I was wondering if you would mind walking me through these reports? I really want to learn more about the business side of things."

I'm finding it difficult to focus on her, but I can sense her interest is genuine. I would normally enjoy the opportunity to do some mentoring, but not right now. "I'm sorry, but I have to be in a meeting in a few minutes. Come by my office tomorrow and I can go over some things with you."

"I don't work tomorrow."

"When do you work next?" I glance around the room, tapping my foot rapidly. I don't see Luke anymore.

"I work next Monday."

"That should work for me. Give a call when you get in, and we can try to set something up."

"That would be great. Thank you."

"No problem." I rush to the door. Someone calls my name, but I pretend I don't hear her. I can't get stuck answering questions when Luke is standing in there. I reach the door. I don't get the opportunity to breathe a sigh of relief though. As I step through it, I'm face to face with the one I'm running from.

"Shit!" I say before I catch myself. I remember where I am and correct myself with a more professional response. "Sorry, excuse me."

"Hi Jess. I saw you trip. Are you okay?" Luke appears more amused than concerned.

"Oh yeah, I'm fine." I anxiously glance around for the person who just called me. I would be happy to answer any questions she may have. I pick up the scent of his cologne. He smells earthy and musky.

"Are you sure? You seem a little frazzled."

I resent the fact that he appears to be enjoying my discomfort. I also resent that my pulse quickens when he directs his attention at me. "Just a busy day at work. How are you?" My attempt to sound casual is completely out of place between the two of us.

"I'm good. I saw you and wanted to say I regretted not getting the opportunity to talk at the reunion." His smile sends a flood of warmth surging through me.

"Oh, that's okay. What are you doing here?" I blurt out the thought dominating my mind.

"I'm meeting a business associate." He leans in, his eyes focused on mine. "Jessica, it's good to see you. And when the time is right, I'd like to speak with you."

I want to ask him what he means by "when the time is right," but I don't get the chance. He strides past me, back into the tasting room.

Chapter 3

After Luke is safely behind the solid tasting room doors, I power-walk back to my office. This, coupled with the adrenaline of seeing him, leaves me breathless and discombobulated.

"What's wrong with you?" Linda stares at me with wide eyes.

"Just saw someone unexpected in the tasting room." My phone rings. "Hello, this is Jessica," I gasp.

"Hi Jessica. It's Mandy from up front. AL Investing is here for your meeting."

Mandy, that's her name. I also forgot about my meeting for a moment. What's the name of the gentleman I'm meeting with? Aaron? I need to pull myself together.

"Please show him to the conference room in the back building and let him know I'll be with him in a couple of minutes. Thanks, Mandy." I hang up. I'm usually not so short with employees, but I only have a few minutes to wipe the sweat off my forehead, gather my wits, and grab the documents and charts I need to present.

This is an important meeting. Aaron contacted me personally, indicating interest in investing in a winery. His name wasn't on the list of investors we originally contacted. When I asked how he heard about us, he said that our contact information had been given to him by a colleague. The winery owner, Mrs. Bianchi, has been meeting with private investors over the past six months. She has big plans to expand and grow the company, but hasn't been able to find the right capital. She's hoping to find someone who shares her passion and sees her vision, not merely someone to serve as an open wallet. Mrs. Bianchi couldn't attend this meeting and has entrusted me to promote the winery as a good investment. I've given this presentation so many times over the last few months, I don't really need to prepare, but I can't go into a meeting in my current state. I take deep breaths while I gather up my reports.

"Wish me luck," I say to Linda as our office door closes behind me. The short walk across the yard gives my heartbeat a few extra minutes to revert to its normal pace.

I stand up straight and smile as I enter the conference room. "Good afternoon, and welcome to Bianchi Winery."

The man sitting at the end of the long mahogany table smiles back at me warmly. He is about my age, maybe a little older, with short, dark brown hair. He is dressed in a polished gray suit with a black tie. He rises from his chair and extends his right hand to me.

"Jessica, thank you for having me." Aaron's handshake is strong.

"Thank you for making the trip down, Mr. Bennet. I think it's valuable to have potential investors do an onsite visit, get the full Bianchi experience." I try to match the firmness of his grip.

"Please, call me Aaron. And I agree. We're happy we could schedule an in-person visit. My partner had to take a phone call. He'll join us in a moment." He smiles again, and it's the kind that instantly puts people at ease. I suppose that smile gives him an advantage in his business dealings.

"I didn't realize your partner was going to be attending our meeting today." I'm relieved I brought an extra set of copies of my reports.

"He travels extensively, and I never know when he'll be available for local meetings. He happened to be in town this week and wanted to join us."

"Local? I thought you're based in San Francisco?"

"We are. We consider anything in California local."

I laugh politely. "I see. Well, great. I'm glad to have the opportunity to speak with both of you."

"Yes. We've both been reading the information packet you sent over. I had a wonderful conversation with Mrs. Bianchi the other day, but I appreciate you making time to go over some of the details with me."

"Of course, I'm happy to elaborate on our plan and answer any questions you may have."

"I have to admit, we're impressed with the proposed direction and vision…" The opening door interrupts Aaron's thoughts. "Jessica, this is my partner, Luke Taylor."

"Nice to meet you, Jessica." Luke walks over and extends a hand, his face void of all recognition.

I'm sure my mouth is hanging open. This must be some twisted joke. Luke can't be his partner. I can't give my pre-sentation to the man who crushed my heart in high school. And to make this nightmare situation even more painful, he's pretending we don't already know each other? I have too many questions and no time for answers. I need to block everything else out except for the business at hand.

"Nice to meet you too, Mr. Taylor." I stand and shake his warm, strong hand.

His eyes sparkle, and a whisper of a smile crosses his lips. I narrow my eyes at him, and he glances over at Aaron. My eyes follow to where Aaron is already pouring over the financial information.

"As I was saying, this investment may work for us, but we would like clarification on some of the details," Aaron continues, unaware of the silent exchange going on between Luke and me.

"Sure. I have prepared some new graphs that better illustrate our projected growth." I slide the additional reports to Aaron and Luke as I take my seat. I focus on Aaron, to better disguise my discomfort.

As the meeting continues, I fall into my rhythm. It helps that Luke is studying the reports and isn't focusing on me. I answer Aaron's questions regarding the winery, its history, and our future goals. Luke doesn't say anything, nor does he look up. I sense the presentation is going well, but the circumstances are so strange, I'm not completely sure. Aaron appears to be receptive to what I'm saying, and I believe I'm making the right impression on him.

Mrs. Bianchi deserves to build the winery she envisions. Beyond being a genuinely kind woman, she has done a lot for me personally. She gave me an opportunity straight out of college and has taught me so much. She believed in me, mentored me, and allowed me to step into a controller role quicker than I could have anywhere else. This position and its security make being a single mother less terrifying. I want this winery and Mrs. Bianchi to be successful. Aaron and Luke are currently my best shot at making this happen.

"In your report, you mention increasing wine production as a direct result of access to additional capital. Obviously an increase in cash would allow for the purchase of equipment necessary to drive that growth. We would like to have a better understanding of how this all comes together. One question that comes to mind: where would the grapes come from?" Aaron is professional and prepared.

"To answer that specific question, we currently harvest a surplus of grapes each year. Historically, we sell this surplus to other wineries, either as whole fruit or bulk wine. Using this fruit to produce more of our own wine would be an option once we have increased production, bottling, and storage capabilities. In addition, we intend to purchase fruit and bulk wine from other wineries. We have already spoken with a local winery in the valley that is willing to sell us their surplus fruit at a reasonable price. In addition, we're working with a mid-sized winery in Napa Valley to determine at what price point they would be willing to sell their bulk wine to us." My confidence continues to grow as the meeting progresses.

"Would it be unrealistic to expect to grow large enough here to avoid having to buy from someone else entirely?" Aaron is flipping back and forth between reports.

"Not necessarily, but it is usually less expensive to buy bulk wine than it is to farm grapes. Mrs. Bianchi takes a lot of pride in the fact that we grow a large percentage of our own grapes, so that won't change. However, the purchase of bulk wine from other vineyards will most likely remain part of our growth strategy. To reach the goal of doubling wine production over the next five years, we will have to employ several different strategies."

"You're asking for a large amount of money. And your plan is fairly aggressive and therefore risky, especially for someone as inexperienced as yourself." Luke unexpectedly joins the conversation, and I consciously stop myself from narrowing my eyes at him.

"I've been with this winery for five years, and I've learned a lot about the business during that time. Mrs. Bianchi has been in this valley for over twenty years. Bianchi Winery has a strong history of growth in this valley and a loyal following. I firmly believe that if we up our game a little, it will pay off."

"Yes, you're clearly very knowledgeable about this business and finances in general, but you have never grown a business of this size, correct?" Luke stares at me unflinchingly.

"I haven't, but that doesn't mean that I don't recognize a good risk when I see one." I return his stare. If he's trying to intimidate me with his challenges, he's failing miserably. My confidence has been ignited, and I'm determined to stand up for myself and this winery.

"Your ability to recognize a worthwhile risk isn't proven." I'm about to say something else in my defense, but Luke raises his hand and continues. "However, I admit I like the overall vision and plan, though I worry about the execution. To be completely honest, in my experience, finance people such as yourself are usually quite conservative. I don't know if you're enough of a risk-taker to follow through and get what you want." He raises an eyebrow.

"I may not be a risk-taker by nature, but Mrs. Bianchi is, and I trust her wisdom and intuition."

"What about you? Do you trust your judgement?" Luke leans back in his chair.

"Luke." Aaron says it like a warning.

"I would feel more comfortable knowing we're entrusting this amount of money to people who can analyze situations and make good decisions." Luke is looking at me like he's hopeful I'll say something.

I'm not sure what exactly he's hoping for, but I've had enough of his games. "Mr. Taylor, Mr. Bennet." I make eye contact with each man as I say their name. "I understand what's at stake for all involved. I also understand risk, perhaps better than most, so while I may err on the side of being cautious, it is that cautiousness that makes me valuable. Relationships, business or otherwise, need balance. Consider me the balance in this equation. I'm the one the risk-takers will have to run their ideas through and convince. I will be the voice of reason. I will act as the brakes of this operation. I'm the person who will prevent us from slamming into a wall going eighty miles an hour."

Luke is looking at me the same way I look at Amelia when she scores a goal during a game.

"I can appreciate that. Some cautiousness is warranted and valuable." Aaron offers some reassurance. I like Aaron so much better than Luke. "It appears that my partner and I have some things to discuss. While we're here, we would like to talk with your winemaker and pick his brain a little."

"Absolutely. His name is Ryan, and he is available at your convenience." I'm grateful this meeting is wrapping up.

We stand, and I shake Aaron's hand first. His phone vibrates in his pocket. "Excuse me, I have to take this." He rushes out without saying another word, and Luke and I are left alone. I distract myself by reorganizing my papers.

"That was a good presentation, Jessica."

"Uh-huh," I mutter without raising my eyes from the table.

"Why are you still using your married name?" When I look up, Luke is frowning at me.

"Seriously? That's what you want to ask me right now?" I snap.

"Are you going back to Adams?"

"What? I don't know. What was that all about anyway? Pretending you didn't know me? Questioning my abilities?" I'm starting to raise my voice, even though I know I shouldn't.

"I want Aaron to make up his mind about the deal without our history clouding his decision, and it's my job to question your experience. This is an investment meeting. You need to be able to answer the hard questions." He shrugs. "I always loved riling you up. You really should be thanking me. Your feistiness made you appear more confident."

"I'm not thanking you for anything." His level of arrogance is truly astounding.

"No need. Seeing your passionate side was thanks enough." Luke smirks, and I want to slap him.

"Passionate? That's an odd word choice for a business meeting." I sound squeaky.

"Passionate is the word that came to mind." His eyes burn. "As for your perceived lack of abilities and experience, I could help you rectify that."

"I do not have a lack of ability, perceived or otherwise. I'm not inexperienced either." I wonder exactly what he's referring to, but I don't dare ask him.

"Sorry about that." Aaron returns and effectively ends my conversation with Luke. "We need to set up that meeting with the winemaker, but I anticipate we can have an answer for you late next week."

"Sounds great. I'll make sure Ryan gets in touch with you before the end of the day." Mrs. Bianchi is going to be thrilled.

Luke is back to pretending not to know me as we wrap things up. They leave, and I'm still reeling from the fact that Luke is even here, let alone the possibility that I may be working with him. Anxiety is already building in my core.

I'm pushing the chairs back under the table when the door opens. I jerk my head up in surprise.

"I forgot something." Luke strides across the room toward me.

I hold my breath. Luke wraps one arm around my waist and tangles his free hand in my hair. Without saying a word, he slams his mouth onto mine. I groan at the sensation of his lips on mine. He slides his tongue into my mouth. He tastes like cinnamon as I kiss him back.

It ends too quickly though. When Luke releases me, we're both panting. He searches my eyes for a moment before quietly heading back to the door.

"I know a good risk when I see one too." Luke turns the doorknob and exits.

Chapter 4

*A*aron and Luke meet with Ryan the next day. I have an appointment scheduled with our CPA firm, so I'm unable to join them. As our winemaker, Ryan paints a more vivid picture of our plan and how everything will be implemented on the operations side. Aaron and Luke are impressed and agree to fund us on the spot. Mrs. Bianchi is so thrilled she gives Ryan and me substantial bonuses.

I celebrate by taking Amelia to the final weekend of the San Diego County Fair. We go on rides until we can't walk straight. We eat cotton candy and popcorn for lunch. I insist on a more substantial meal of giant slices of sourdough bread topped with cheese and pepperoni for dinner. We try chocolate-covered bacon and fried Twinkies for dessert. We both enjoy the former more than expected and the latter less. We laugh until our stomachs hurt. I let her play as many of the overpriced carnival games as she wants. I lug around the giant stuffed snake she somehow wins. She falls asleep on the car ride home, and I smile the entire way.

Luke does not contact me after our meeting, and I find myself dealing solely with Aaron. Luke's absence makes it easier to convince myself I can see him in a business setting and not let it affect my work. After several weeks without contact from him, I berate myself for overthinking everything. The kiss wasn't anything serious, and I feel foolish for even wondering what it could possibly have meant.

The more I consider it, the angrier I get. I'm angry with Luke for assuming he could kiss me like that, but I'm also angry with myself for kissing him back. I'm mortified that I enjoyed it, and that it has since entered my dreams more than once. I rack my brain, trying to come up with a way to rationalize my reaction to it. I settle on the idea that it was so sudden and unexpected I didn't have time to think. It was only familiarity that made me enjoy it, much less allow it. It's like when you hear an old song on the radio. You're excited to hear it because it carries some nostalgia, but after a few more seconds of listening, you realize it's actually not a very good song after all. Luke is merely an old, bad song.

His unpredictable attitude toward me is confusing, but I don't have to let his fluctuations affect me. I've made up my mind. Nothing good can come from getting mixed up with Luke Taylor again.

The remainder of spring flies by, and summer arrives, threatening to do the same. Plans for the expansion roll forward, keeping me busy. I spend as much time as possible with Amelia. I take her to the beach or we swim in the backyard most weekends she's with me. Grant takes her to Orlando on the trip we had planned as a family. He sends me a text and invites me to join them. I don't respond, and he doesn't ask again.

I use the week they are gone to move into our new rental. I wasn't ready to commit to the purchase of a new home when I moved out of the house I shared with Grant. After several months of staying at my mom's house in Rancho

Bernardo, I finally found a great little place with a pool near Amelia's school.

We celebrate Amelia's eighth birthday with a pool party in the backyard. I include Grant to be polite, and much to my dismay, he accepts the invitation. Thankfully, he keeps his distance and only stays for a short time. I hope someday we can be one of those friendly co-parenting couples, but I'm not ready yet. Peaceful coexistence is all I can currently muster.

I also spend as much time as possible with my girlfriends and my mom. I eventually share with each of them the stories of the reunion and of Luke becoming an investor at the winery. Knowing our history, my mom is concerned. She always liked Luke, but she saw the devastation he caused too. My divorce isn't even final yet, and everyone is beginning to get over my painful reaction to it. She's worried about me and about what another heartbreak would do to me. I'm worried too. My girlfriends, Vivien and Emily, express similar concerns, but are quieter about them than my mother is. I assure them all that I have no interest in Luke.

After a full summer, we're all ready to get back into a normal routine. Amelia returned to school a few weeks ago and we have begun a new harvest season in the vineyard. I love this time of year. It has always felt like a time of new beginnings to me.

Even though fall is approaching, the thermometer indicates summer won't leave without a fight. I pull on a pair of shorts, flip-flops, and a Bianchi Winery shirt. I normally avoid having to be at winery events on my days off, but today is my favorite event of the year, the annual harvest celebration. It's a family event at the winery, with people of all ages participating in various games and contests. The main attraction of the day is the grape stomp competition. People jump up and down and attempt to squash grapes in a barrel as quickly as possible. It's as entertaining to watch as it is to participate in.

We went as a family last year. I still laugh at the pictures of Amelia, legs stained purple, after her turn stomping. I'll miss that this year. This is Grant's weekend with her. We've talked very little over the past few months. I'm afraid that if we were to talk more, I would only scream at him. That is not something I ever want to do in front of Amelia, so I try to stick to texting and conversation requiring yes or no answers only. I can't avoid him forever, but it's working for now.

The theme for this year's celebration is "crush." The winery staff, including me, are wearing black T-shirts with the Bianchi Winery logo and various sayings such as *Crushing Hard at Bianchi Winery* and *I Crushed it at Bianchi Winery*. The shirts are meant to be playful and evoke thoughts of wine and love. At least that's what Monica, our director of marketing, said at one of the planning meetings.

My shirt reads *Everyone Remembers Their First Crush*. "Crush" is a twisted word. It can describe an intense passion or a hurtful demolition. How can one shirt cause me to simultaneously think of the two men I'm trying not to think about? I hate this shirt, which in this moment, makes me kind of hate Monica too.

"Hi Jessica."

Speak of the devil. "Hi Monica."

She approaches me from the front of the lawn, where the events staff is setting up various tents and tables. "You're working the sign-in table today, right?"

"That was my plan since Linda couldn't be here today. Unless you need me somewhere else?" I want to add that perhaps I can do something that would require I change out of this shirt, but I don't.

"No, that would be great. Oh, and I saw your name on the list for the employee competition." This is news to me, since I didn't sign up to participate this year, but a team must have been short a person, and I got added.

"I didn't know I was competing today, but just put me on whatever team you need me on." The grape stomp is a messy event. Maybe my shirt will get ruined.

"Thank you so much. I owe you one."

You have no idea, Monica.

I work the sign-in table with Ryan. He checks in guests who have prepaid online while I collect payment from guests registering today. Two hours go by quickly. Ryan and I pack up our table as Mrs. Bianchi begins to give instructions to the crowd. I glance at the podium. Standing to the right of the podium are Luke and Aaron. I was told they weren't going to be here today.

I take a deep breath and sigh as we move the table into one of the storage closets. Today just got more interesting.

When we step back into the crowd, Mrs. Bianchi's voice booms once again through the speakers. "On your mark, get set, crush!"

The air is filled with laughter, squeals, and hollering as the teams egg on their stomping members. In this moment,

I wish I had signed up to be a team judge, because Mrs. Bianchi is heading directly toward me, and Luke and Aaron are with her.

"Jessica, Ryan, there you are! Look who decided to join us today," Mrs. Bianchi calls out when she is still several feet away.

"Nice to see you both again." Ryan shakes hands with our two new investors.

"Good morning." I offer my hand as well. Luke's handshake is no different than Aaron's, yet somehow it seems less friendly.

The men make small talk about the event and the summer-like weather. I try to relax and follow the conversation even though it has not escaped my attention that Luke has not looked at me once since shaking my hand.

"I like the shirts the staff are wearing. Very clever." Luke doesn't turn his eyes toward me when he says it, but I know the comment and the smirk on his face are directed at me.

Now I really hate this shirt and all it implies. Most of all, I hate standing in front of him wearing this shirt.

"Aren't they great? Such a fun play on words. And I mean, who doesn't remember their first crush, right?" Everyone nods in agreement, except Luke. I like the idea that I may have made him uncomfortable.

"I certainly remember mine," Ryan responds. "That girl broke my heart."

Aaron shakes his head and laughs. "Mine too. She broke up with me and started dating my friend…on Valentine's Day."

"I guess I was fortunate, because my husband was my first crush." Mrs. Bianchi is wearing the same expression of adoration she always wears when she talks of Mr. Bianchi.

"You are one of the lucky ones," I tell her sincerely.

"I know Luke remembers his first love." Aaron gives no indication he knows he's referring to me.

Luke stares hard at Aaron. After a second, he smiles. "She is definitely unforgettable. Unfortunately, I was not one of the lucky ones though."

"Another broken heart, huh?" Mrs. Bianchi sighs.

I can't help but huff out a cynical breath. The men turn their attention to me.

"What about you, Jessica? Was Grant your first love?" Ryan asks.

"No, he wasn't," I answer shortly. This day just keeps getting better.

"And?" Ryan pushes. I shoot him a dirty look, and he responds with an apologetic grimace.

"And nothing. Classic story of the girl being more invested in the relationship than the boy." I'm careful not to make eye contact with Luke. A knot forms in my stomach.

Aaron changes the subject by asking Ryan a question about which grapes are being used for the competition. I should be grateful that Luke is ignoring me. Instead I feel deprived. My mind wanders until I hear Mrs. Bianchi's voice again.

"I signed you both up for the winery competition. I hope you don't mind." She is addressing Luke and Aaron.

"Great. We'd be honored. I have to warn you though that Luke is very competitive." Aaron grins at her.

"Aaron is exaggerating. I just try to do my best." Luke wears a hint of a smile on his lips. He is keenly aware of how competitive he is.

"No, I'm not. I once witnessed a very heated game of Monopoly between my wife and this one." Aaron points at Luke.

"She didn't want to negotiate a fair sales price for any of her properties." Luke shrugs.

"They finally ended the game after midnight when I kicked Luke out of the house."

They laugh, and Luke shakes his head at Aaron. I resist the urge to share my own stories about Luke's competitive drive. Like the hours he spent at the batting cages or the time he insisted we stay up all night studying for our chemistry final. I ended up with the higher score, and although he was happy for me, I could tell he was disappointed in himself.

I take an opportunity to glance at him while he's laughing and not paying attention to me. He's so handsome it's hard to look away. His laughter makes his blue eyes sparkle. His eyes were always one of my favorite features. They change color depending on what he's wearing and what the weather is like. On this sunny day, he has on a royal-blue T-shirt, and his eyes have taken on a sapphire hue.

"The departments form teams of three and compete against each other for bragging rights. It gets pretty competitive," Mrs. Bianchi explains. "Ryan needs a third person on his winemaking team, and one of you can join the team with Jessica and myself."

"Perfect. I volunteer to help the winemaking team." Luke walks over to stand next to Ryan.

"Sounds good." Ryan nods.

"Aaron, that means you're with us."

I should be relieved Luke isn't on my team. Instead I notice a feeling of disappointment.

The first round of competition is wrapping up, so we all walk over to the barrels. There will be additional rounds of guest contests throughout the day, but we try to break it up by planning other events. The guests always enjoy watching the employee round, which is next. There are eight teams this year, but I would be willing to bet the winemaking team will win. Ryan and his assistant, Simon, usually do well during the stomp. With Luke being added to their team, they might be unbeatable.

The rules are simple. The competition is a relay, with each member of the team required to get in a half barrel and stomp on grapes for two minutes. The resulting juice flows out of a spout into a measuring cup. The team that produces the most juice in six minutes wins. Several winery employees serve as judges. Mrs. Bianchi wasn't kidding when she said this was a competitive contest.

Monica announces the event over the PA system, and the crowd grows. Mr. Bianchi approaches with the grown Bianchi children and their families in tow. The winery teams choose their barrels and prepare for the event. Trash talking and taunting between the teams begin.

Ryan's team is next to us. Ryan will go first, followed by Simon, with Luke going last. We have decided Mrs. Bianchi will go first, followed by me, with Aaron going last.

The whistle blows, and Mrs. Bianchi and Ryan climb into the barrel and start stomping. It is extremely noisy as all the teams cheer on their members.

The whistle blows again. Mrs. Bianchi climbs out, and I climb in. Once I have my footing, I stomp as fast and as hard as I can. I glance at the other barrel to see Simon looking very determined.

The whistle blows again. I climb out, and Aaron climbs in. My foot twists on the slippery grass, and I fall to one knee.

"Are you all right?" Ryan rushes over and grabs my arm to help me up.

"I'm fine." I wave him off. "Just clumsy." My ankle is throbbing, but I don't want anyone to know.

I balance on one foot as I watch the final minute of the competition. Luke and Aaron never even glance at each other as they furiously stomp the grapes in their barrels. The final whistle blows, and the judges grab the measuring cups in order to determine a winner. Luke and Aaron step out of their barrels and shake hands.

"Jessica, are you okay?" Aaron asks as everyone hoses grape juice off their legs and feet.

"Yeah. Not a big deal." I try to minimize Aaron's concern.

"Let me see." Luke bends down in front of me and takes my ankle in his warm hands. It feels good until he applies a little pressure. I wince.

"Probably a sprain. Do you have a first-aid kit around here?" Luke directs his question at Mrs. Bianchi.

"Really, I'm fine," I say forcefully.

Luke stands and takes a step back. "Can you walk on it?"

I take a step, but hobble from the pain.

"It's sore, but I'm sure I'll live." I try to lighten the mood and my embarrassment.

"Each office has a first-aid kit," Mrs. Bianchi says.

"Great. I played a lot of ball when I was younger and have taken care of many sprains. I'll get this wrapped up."

"Really…" I start to resist again, but Luke shoots me a look that makes me stop.

"Where is your office?" Luke asks pointedly.

I point across the lawn. "In that building." I give in to my fate.

"Here, I'll carry you." Luke starts toward me with his arms outstretched.

There is no way in hell I'm letting him carry me. "I'll hop." I say it with enough seriousness that Luke lowers his arms.

"Jessica, it's too far to hop. Let him help you," Mrs. Bianchi pleads.

Ryan hurries to my side. "Put your arm over my shoulder."

"I got her." Luke doesn't ask. He grabs my left arm and swings it over his shoulder.

At this point I will make more of a scene if I continue to protest, so I don't. We're about halfway to my office when it becomes apparent this isn't working. Luke is taller than me, and the height difference is too much. This time he doesn't ask before scooping me up in his arms.

He doesn't say anything as we continue on to my office. I can't help but breathe in his cologne, and it messes with my thoughts. I punch in my code to unlock the door, and he carries me into my office.

"Where's the first-aid kit?" He glances around the room.

I point to the metal box hanging on the wall.

Luke takes out an instant cold pack and an elastic bandage. He kneels in front me and holds the cold pack on my ankle for a few minutes.

"Why do you do that?" he asks, eyes focused on my swollen ankle.

"I didn't mean to. I should have been more careful on the slick grass."

"Not that. Why do you pretend you're fine when you're not?"

"I don't know what you're talking about," I lie. It's always been a reflex of mine not to burden others.

Luke doesn't press the issue. He wraps my ankle with the bandage. He's gentle, but every time his hands touch my bare skin, shivers run through me. He peers up at me. "Don't look at me like that." Luke stands.

"Excuse me?" I sense my cheeks flushing.

"Don't look at me like I can fix everything." Luke tilts his head down.

"I'm not asking you to fix anything. You were the one who insisted on wrapping my ankle, and now you're pissed off about it?"

"I'm not talking about your ankle, and you know it."

"Actually, I don't know what you're talking about. I don't know what you're doing. You change how you treat me by the minute. First you pretend not to know me, then you kiss me, then you avoid me for weeks, then when I do see you again, you're back to acting like you don't know me. Then you insist on helping me when you don't really want to." I move my arms excitedly to illustrate my point. "You don't make any sense. Pick a lane."

He runs his hands through his hair and stares up at the ceiling.

"You're right, I do need to pick a lane." He abruptly turns and walks out of my office.

I hobble back outside after several minutes of resting my ankle. Ryan, Simon, and Luke won the competition. Everyone is mingling and drinking wine. Except for Luke. Apparently the lane he picked sent him back to San Francisco early.

Chapter 5

Several weeks after the harvest celebration, the first phase of the expansion plan is officially drafted, and Mrs. Bianchi plans a party to get all of the investors together. Aaron and Luke aren't the winery's only investors, but they are the newest and largest. The evening will be a celebration, but it will also be an opportunity to present the completed plans and spark some additional excitement about the project. Luke indicated he is unable to attend, which means my evening will be enjoyable and uncomplicated.

It's Thursday, and since it will be Grant's weekend with Amelia, he agrees to keep her an extra night. Honestly, his guilt makes him agree to anything I ask these days. He's lucky it's not in my nature to abuse this power. Amelia staying at Grant's tonight means tomorrow will be the first time I haven't dropped her off at school. It pains me how she has to split her time between us. It leads to all of us missing out on some things.

Since I don't have to pick Amelia up from school today, there really isn't any reason I have to go home before the party. It's easier to bring a change of clothes and get ready in the bridal cottage, a space available for women getting married on the property. It's a quaint little room, decorated in floral and lace.

Once I'm ready for the party, I return to my office to finish writing an email to Monica regarding a press release related to the expansion. When I log into my computer, I see an email from Aaron.

To: Jessica Rogers
From: Aaron Bennet
Subject: Investor Dinner

Hello Jessica,

I apologize, but I won't be able to attend the dinner tonight. My mother is in the hospital. She should be okay, but I need to fly home to go see her. Please forgive my last-minute cancelation. I'll try to make it down there again soon. I've sent an email directly to Mrs. Bianchi letting her know as well.

Aaron Bennet
Partner, AL Investing

I'm disappointed. I enjoy working with Aaron and was looking forward to seeing him tonight.

To: Aaron Bennet
From: Jessica Rogers
Subject: Re: Investor Dinner

Aaron,

I'm sorry you're unable to attend this evening, but I completely understand. I hope your mom makes a full recovery. Of course you're welcome to visit the winery anytime. Let me know when you plan to come to Temecula again, and I'll make myself available for lunch.

Jessica Rogers
Controller, Bianchi Winery

I press send and finish typing my email to Monica. I'm about to shut down my computer when a notification pops up indicating Aaron has already replied.

To: Jessica Rogers
From: Aaron Bennet
Subject: Investor Dinner

Jessica,

Thank you, I will. I forgot to mention that Luke will be attending after all, so AL will still be represented. Hope tonight goes well.

Aaron Bennet
Partner, AL Investing

Luke and I are professionals. We will find a way to put our past behind us and work together. Keeping our distance from each other seems to be the best way we deal with each other, so that's what we'll have to do.

I shut down my computer and make one last assessment of my appearance in the mirror hanging on the back of my office door. The curls I placed in my hair this morning have relaxed into loose waves. My navy lace dress flatters my figure, but earlier I had debated whether it was too low cut for a work function. I decided it was professional enough, but now that I know Luke is coming, I feel self-conscious.

The dinner is being held in the barrel room. When I walk in, I'm taken aback by how beautiful it is. The room is set up with long banquet tables covered in white linens, white china, and sparkling crystal stemware. Each table is elegantly decorated with an abundance of white flowers in vases of varying heights and white candles. A jazz band is setting up in one corner of the room, and the service staff is finalizing the setting by lighting additional candles that have been perched on the wine barrels that line the walls. There are place cards on the tables. I quickly find mine and see I'm sitting next to Luke. I glance around, realize no one is paying attention to me, and switch cards before anyone takes notice.

Mr. and Mrs. Bianchi enter the room as I walk away from the scene of the crime.

"Jessica! How lovely to see you, my dear." Mr. Bianchi embraces me and kisses me on the cheek.

"Mr. Bianchi, you're more handsome every time I see you." The Bianchis must be in their sixties, and they are an elegant couple. She is a classic beauty and is always impeccably put together. Tonight, she is wearing a stunning emerald-green dress with a matching necklace. Her long gray hair is swept up in a French twist. I wonder if I'll ever have enough confidence to let my hair go completely gray. Mr. Bianchi looks effortless in a dignified black suit. They co-own the winery, but she is more involved in the day-to-day operations. He prefers to remain behind the scenes and handle more of their personal investments and finances.

"Ah, I'm an old man, but you appear to be aging backward."

"Quit flirting with the employees," Mrs. Bianchi teases. "We need to find her a young, sexy man."

"Hey, I'm sexy." Mr. Bianchi smiles warmly at her.

"Yes, you are." Mrs. Bianchi kisses him on the cheek. "But you're old and mine." She winks at me.

"True. Sorry, Jessica, we will just have to find you some other hunk," Mr. Bianchi says, and we all laugh.

"Okay, but only if I can have something close to what you two have." I smile.

When I got pregnant with Amelia my junior year of college, I wasn't sure what that meant for my education or future. My mom and Grant's mom felt it was important I finish school, so they helped as much as they could while still holding us responsible for our family. I worked hard, but I cut back when I needed to. Because of their help, it only took me one extra semester to obtain my bachelor's degree. After graduation, I was nervous about being a mom with a new career and how I would balance everything. Grant was still in dental school, so we couldn't afford for me to be a stay-at-home mom at that point. He encouraged me to go on interviews and keep an open mind. Bianchi Winery was my first interview, and I immediately knew I wanted the job. I started as a staff accountant working under a very smart and talented woman. Mrs. Bianchi took an interest in me and included me in meetings and sent me to industry conferences when she could. With their support, I worked hard and learned as much about the business as I could. Two years later, when Susan retired, Mrs.

Bianchi promoted me to controller. This place has become my second home. Mrs. Bianchi cried with me when I told her about Grant's affair.

Mrs. Bianchi says, "You really have done an amazing job helping me secure the investors we need. I'm going to give a small presentation tonight, but I want you to relax and enjoy the evening."

She makes me blush with her kind words.

"You've earned it, and I am so proud of you," Mr. Bianchi adds, and tears well in my eyes. He is the closest thing I've had to a father figure.

"Thank you, I will. But please let me know if I can help with anything."

"Go get a glass of wine." Mrs. Bianchi squeezes my arm as she walks past me to greet the guests who have started to arrive.

Ryan enters through a back door and sneaks up behind me. "Hey there." He taps me on the shoulder.

"Ryan! You startled me." I actually jump a little.

"Sorry." Ryan frowns at me. "Let me get you a glass of wine to make amends."

"Sounds good. What are we pouring tonight?"

"The new Syrah, the Cab, and the Vernaccia blend."

"Well, you're the expert."

"I vote for the Syrah tonight. It turned out really good." Ryan always lights up when he talks about wine.

"Perfect." I wait while Ryan asks the bar server to pour us two glasses of the deep-crimson wine.

As I'm waiting, I inadvertently eavesdrop on the conversation of two women standing next to the bar. They appear to be in their early-twenties. Their giggling and animated voices are hard to ignore. One is filling the other in on an awkward date she recently had with a young man from her economics class when they suddenly start whispering. Feeling a little let down that I'm not going to get to hear the end of the story, I follow their sight line to see what has caught their attention.

A man in a navy suit has walked into the room. He is wearing a crisp white shirt under his suit, with the top button undone. It's an effortlessly sexy style, and he carries it well. They, along with several other females in the room, have taken notice of the self-assured, beautiful stranger.

I see the handsome exterior, but I also see the danger lurking underneath. This man is not a stranger to me, and I know firsthand the consequences of falling for him. This is the man I have promised my mother, my friends, and myself I am going to stay away from.

I successfully avoid Luke during cocktail hour by engaging in conversation with other guests and otherwise pretending to answer texts. Every time I steal a glance around the room, I find Luke engaged with an ever-growing circle of people. Maybe he's avoiding me too. Maybe tonight won't be complicated after all. I'm internally congratulating us on finding a way to navigate the situation when the announcement to take our seats for dinner is given.

Ryan pulls out my chair for me and I take my seat next to him. My eyes grow wide when Luke walks over and sits directly across from him.

"Good evening," Luke says. He must have made some of his own adjustments to the seating arrangements. "I'm glad we're sitting by each other during dinner. It'll give us a chance to catch up."

I take a big drink of wine.

The table is engaged in lively, wine-fueled small talk, so no one takes notice when Luke leans across to mouth to me that I look beautiful. I'm not sure if it's the wine, the compliment, or the fact that Luke is staring at me in a very seductive way, but I experience a rush of warmth. This is not the professional lane I thought we were planning to stay in.

After everyone has settled in, Mrs. Bianchi gives a short but inspired presentation of the finalized expansion plans. I scan the room to read reactions. Everyone appears genuinely excited and engaged. It is my turn to be proud of her.

The waitstaff delivers our salads, and Luke's attention turns to a conversation Ryan is having about the winemaking process. Luke is polite and listens patiently, but I know him too well. I sense there is something he doesn't like about Ryan.

Being this close to Luke is proving once again to be more difficult than I anticipated. He makes me feel things I don't want to, things that make me uneasy. I disguise my struggle by engaging in a lively conversation with Mrs. Everett. She is a longtime friend of the Bianchis, and I always enjoy our interactions.

We're halfway through dinner when Ryan grabs my elbow. He asks if I would like another glass of the Syrah. It's subtle, but I catch Luke's fist tighten as his eyes narrow slightly. I blink, and Luke has already hidden his reaction. He continues to talk with the young woman sitting next to him. She is one of the women from the conversation I listened in on during cocktail hour. She laughs too loudly at everything Luke says and touches his arm frequently. I return my attention to Mrs. Everett.

Unfortunately, the conversation is short-lived when Mrs. Everett excuses herself to go say hello to another guest. As a result, I'm forced to reengage with the rest of the table. The topic of conversation has turned to dating. I can't think of a topic I would less like to discuss in present company.

"It's so hard to meet good men these days," says the woman next to Luke. It's such an uninteresting thing to say that I start to roll my eyes, then I remember where I am and stop. I reach my hand up to my eye and pretend like I have something caught in it. I don't fool Luke, who grins at me.

"It's hard to find a good woman too, but they are out there. You have to keep your eyes open and be patient. Dare to see people in a different light. Sometimes the right person is closer than you think." He's quick about it, but Ryan's glance at me doesn't go unnoticed, not by me or Luke.

"Finding a good woman isn't hard. Holding on to her is a different matter. Men tend to mess things up, and women tend to not know what they want." Luke stares at me.

Ryan nods at Luke. "I agree. Women say they want a nice guy, but when they have one, they don't appreciate him."

Luke stares Ryan down. "I don't think we do agree. A woman doesn't need a nice boy. She needs someone who will treat her with respect but who is man enough to satisfy all her needs." He turns to me, eyes full of heat.

Mrs. Everett, who has since returned to the table, chokes on her wine. The woman sitting next to Luke widens her eyes. Ryan is clearly intimidated by Luke's intensity and laughs nervously. I stare back at Luke and mouth *stop* to him.

"I think we can all agree dating is hard, and good wine makes it a little easier." Ryan raises his glass to toast and attempts to lighten the mood. Several of us, but not Luke, raise our glasses too. Ryan's attempt is successful, and several conversations spring up, centering on topics like the weather, the upcoming holidays, and what football teams are showing promise this year.

I'm defending my position that the Green Bay Packers have the talent to go all the way this season with Mr. Wallace, another investor. He is knowledgeable about the sport, and I start to relax, enjoying the dark chocolate cake that has been served for dessert.

Ryan taps my arm to gain my attention once again. When I turn to face him, he places his hand on mine on the table. The gesture feels too intimate coming from him, and it makes me uncomfortable. I attempt to appear casual when I pull it back into my lap.

Ryan shakes off the rejection. "I was hoping I can steal you for a dance later."

"We'll see." Dancing with Ryan wouldn't be a wise idea. I would tell him so, if we didn't have an audience. Luke is listening to our exchange. I turn my attention back to a conversation at the other side of the table.

The band ups its tempo as the waitstaff attends to the tables once again, offering to bring coffee and tea. Mr. and Mrs. Bianchi take to the dance floor, and several other couples follow suit.

Luke's voice startles me. "Jessica. Accompany me out onto the dance floor?" He is already standing when I look over.

Although he poses it as a question, his eyes tell me it's more of a demand. He's an investor, and I'm at a business function, so I won't decline even though I don't particularly like having him tell me what to do. The woman who has been trying to capture his attention all night gives a deflated sigh, and I hear her ask Ryan if he would like to dance as I rise and set my napkin on the table.

We walk to the center of the room and join the other couples on the dance floor. The jazz music playing is seductive and sensual. Combined with the wine, it's creating an environment that is not appropriate for me to be interacting with Luke in.

Luke grasps my right hand and wraps his free arm around my waist. He pulls me closer. My pulse quickens. Luke holds me firmly, and I instinctively follow his lead. I release the breath I didn't realize I was holding.

"What's going on between you and the jellyfish?" he asks after a few seconds that feels like hours.

"Jellyfish?" I lean back to see his face.

He nods toward Ryan, who is dancing with the woman from the table. "No backbone."

"What do you mean?" I peer over his shoulder when looking into his eyes feels too intimate.

"That guy is a total wimp. He's clearly interested in you, but he's afraid to stake his claim. He just let me take you away."

"First of all, you did not take me away from anyone. I'm dancing with a business associate at a business dinner because you asked me to. It would've been rude to say no."

"Did you want to say no?" Luke interrupts.

"Second, I don't want anyone to 'stake a claim' on me. Sorry to disappoint your overactive imagination, but Ryan is just a friend." I keep my voice low. I don't want to draw attention to whatever is brewing between us.

"If Ryan was my friend and ever looked at me the way he looks at you, we would have to have a long talk about boy parts and girl parts and what parts I'm interested in seeing without any clothes on."

"You really are something else, you know that?" I know how Ryan has acted this evening, and I will have to straighten some things out with him, but I have no interest in hearing Luke's take on things.

"Come on, Jessica. That guy has been eye-fucking you all night." He doesn't hide the frustration in his voice. "If I were him, I wouldn't have given you the opportunity to dance with someone else."

"Ryan is more respectful than that. He wouldn't act like such an ass," I snap back with more emotion than I mean to.

"Ryan is a coward. A man who doesn't know how to get what he wants."

"Right now you're acting like a man who wants to get slapped." I grit my teeth.

"Seriously, that guy could never give you what you need."

"You have no idea what I need. Since this dance was some misguided effort on your part to prove something to Ryan, we're done here." I try to pull away, but Luke holds me against him.

He leans down to whisper, "Oh, but I do know what you need." His breath on my ear gives me the chills. "And I never said I asked you to dance for Ryan's sake. That was merely a fortunate side effect. I asked you to dance because I wanted to."

We move without talking for a few seconds. It feels right and wrong at the same time. I notice Luke's body relax.

"What are you doing, Luke?" I sigh.

"I haven't been fair to you. I've sent some mixed signals." His voice hums softly in my ear. "I didn't know what to make of the emotions seeing you again stirred up in me. It started at the reunion, when I found out you were getting divorced. You walked away that night, and I couldn't stop thinking about you. I couldn't make myself stay away."

"Is that why you showed up here? You tracked me down?"

"You really think it was a coincidence I ended up here two weeks after the reunion?"

"I haven't thought much about it." A lie.

Luke laughs softly. I hate that he finds it funny when he reads through my bullshit. "Don't get me wrong. Aaron and I are always searching for new companies to invest in, so when I found out where you worked, the pieces started fitting together. I told Aaron about the opportunity and went to that meeting thinking it could potentially be a good business opportunity. I thought it could also be a chance at closure for us. But I couldn't resist. I had to kiss you."

"Yes, and then you disappeared."

"I was trying to do what I thought was right. I convinced myself I got it out of my system and we could just work together. I came to the harvest event with every intention of keeping things professional. I realized two things that day. First, I did not like the way Ryan looked at you."

"Jealously is a very unbecoming quality."

"Second, I realized that it was going to be impossible to keep things professional between us."

"Excuse me, I have been professional. Don't confuse your issues with mine."

"Jess, you forget how well I know you."

"Knew me," I correct.

"You haven't changed all that much. Your heart still races every time I touch you. I felt it that day in the conference room and when I carried you to your office, and I can feel it now."

I unsuccessfully try to pull away again. "My heart is racing because I'm angry."

"After that day in your office, my plan was to stay away again, since I can't seem to keep my hands off you. It took everything in me not to kiss you again."

I remind myself to breathe.

"You were right to tell me to pick a lane. I planned on stepping back and letting Aaron handle this investment. I figured that would make it easier for us, but someone once told me that the easy road is for average people, and I'm not average. It kind of stuck with me." He's using my own words against me, words I said to encourage him to pursue his dream of playing professional baseball.

"Sometimes the easy road is the right road."

"I'm going to be blunt. I know you want me, and I definitely want you. I also know you well enough to know you're fighting those feelings because they scare you."

Damn right they scare me. Our high school relationship almost destroyed me. "We work together now. When I said pick a lane, I meant the one where we interact on a professional level. I'm sure we can figure out a way to coexist. Or if it's easier, we can avoid each other."

"Those aren't options for me anymore. You're too bright. Looking at you is like driving into the afternoon sun. I get blinded and swerve out of my lane every time." He brushes my hair back and places his lips below my ear. "You look amazing tonight."

"That's it, we're done here." I summon every ounce of self-preservation I have and pull away. I need to shut this down before he derails me and my career in one night. I need to walk away while I still can. This time when I push away from Luke, he lets me go.

I walk, as quickly as I can in my three-inch heels, out the doors of the barrel room and back toward my office. The cool autumn air feels refreshing as it dances across my overheated skin. I hear footsteps behind me, footsteps that are quicker than mine. As I round the corner of the warehouse, a warm hand encircles my wrist. Luke pulls me back toward him and leans me up against the side of the building. His hands shoot up to my neck, and he lifts my head so I'm forced to look into his eyes. His midnight eyes are mesmerizing. I lick my lips, and he accepts the invitation to taste them. His lips are soft, but the kiss is not. He still tastes like cinnamon, but mixed with wine this time. He tangles his hands in my curls and pulls. My head tilts back, and my mouth opens wider. He uses the opportunity to deepen our kiss. My mind is swirling. Oh my, this feels good. No, wait. This can't happen. This is a mistake.

I come to my senses and push him away. "Stop doing that," I say sternly between pants.

He appears shocked. I assume not many women push Luke Taylor away. He recovers quickly though. "I'm not ever going to be sorry for that kiss. I don't understand why you're resisting so hard."

"Because this is not going to happen." Even though it needs to be said, it pains me to say it.

He cocks his head. "That didn't sound very convincing to me. Did it to you?"

"You are infuriating. It doesn't matter if it sounds convincing. It's reality."

"Hmm, interesting." He's grinning like he knows something I don't.

I know better, but I bite anyway. "What's interesting?"

He takes a step closer. "Interesting word choice, reality. A word I don't believe you're all that interested in."

"Of course I am." I sound timid. I suspect I'm about to step into his trap.

"You're trying to control the situation. But since you brought it up, let's talk about it. The reality of the situation is that we are going to be working together. The reality is that I can't resist you, and every time I come near you, you get flustered trying to resist me." His eyes are full of desire. "Come back to my hotel with me."

"What? No! Absolutely not." My voice is so high-pitched, I don't recognize it.

"Why?" Luke appears as calm and undeterred as I've ever seen him.

"What do you mean, why?"

"We both know it's not because you don't want to."

I wish he would stop smiling at me like that. "I can't."

"Pretty sure you can. We're adults, we're both unattached, and we're unmistakably attracted to each other."

"I'm sure what's-her-name inside would jump at your invitation." I'm hoping a diversion will buy me some time to come up with a good excuse, because the more he talks, the more I'm considering leaving with him.

He scrunches his brow. "I wouldn't be out here with you if I had any interest in what's-her-name. I want you."

"Well, maybe you can't have me."

"I'm simply trying to get you to see what I see, and you will when you're ready." He smiles at me in a way that warms my whole body. "It's getting late, and I have an early day tomorrow. I would love nothing more than for you to leave with me right now."

"Not happening." I try to sound surer of my answer than I am.

"Perhaps not tonight, but this is happening." He kisses my cheek, letting his lips linger long enough to remind me this isn't merely a friendly gesture.

I close my eyes as a shiver runs down my neck. When I open them, he is already walking away.

Chapter 6

After some reflection, and a few pints of rocky road ice cream, I decide I made the right decision when I didn't leave with Luke after the investor dinner. The next week I catch up with Aaron, who tells me his mother is doing much better. I am relieved for him. I also find out through Aaron that Luke is traveling again, this time to the East Coast. Luke stays in contact all week by texting, calling, and emailing. I stick to purely professional responses, which is particularly challenging when he tells me he hopes I wear the navy dress to the next work function.

I make it a point to schedule a lunch with Ryan. Before I can even bring it up, he apologizes for any inappropriate behavior from the dinner. I assure him he doesn't owe me an apology, but I need to make sure he understands my feelings for him are purely friendship based. We agree that our friendship is important and intact. I change the subject when he questions me about Luke's possessive behavior from that night.

By the end of the week, my life has fallen back into a smooth routine. Amelia came to me a couple days ago and begged for a sleepover with her best friend, Sam. I hate to miss out on any time with her but decide it's good for her and me to have some time with our friends. I make plans with Vivien and Emily after work. We have decided to meet at Lucky Stone, an Irish pub that features local bands on the weekends. We've only been there once before but found the place charming.

I arrive on time, but true to form, Vivien is already there, reading something on her phone while she waits for us. Emily won't arrive for another fifteen minutes and will be apologetic that she is late. That's the thing about good friends; we know each other's quirks and love each other more because of them.

"Hey, Viv!" She abandons whatever she was reading to stand up and give me a hug.

"Hey, stranger!"

"Ugh, I know. Work has been crazy the last few weeks, but I don't want to talk about that tonight. How are you?"

I pour myself a glass of my favorite zinfandel from the bottle Vivien has already started on, and we catch each other up on the less exciting details of our lives. I tell her about Amelia starting third grade and already establishing a reputation as this year's class clown. She tells me about her new group of students and how busy her new schedule is making her. The private school she works at talked her into running the yearbook this year. She talks about how demanding it is and how much time she is spending on it, but I can tell she's enjoying the challenge. I decide to wait until Emily gets here to tell them the latest about Luke.

"Sorry I'm late. Of course my boss had just one more thing I had to do before leaving." Emily offers the apology we knew she would.

"When are you leaving that place?" Vivien asks. We have heard about Emily's boss from hell for several years, and he sounds like a nightmare. He owns the roofing company where

Emily is the office manager. Besides engaging in unethical business practices, he has a temper and has yelled at everyone, including Emily.

"I've looked. Unfortunately Max knows he's an asshole on some level, so he overpays people to get them to stay. I would have to take a pretty big pay cut if I leave."

"It might be worth it," I suggest.

"Maybe. Anyway, who has something more exciting to talk about?"

"I do. I saw Luke again."

"And?" Emily eyes me suspiciously while Vivien pours her a glass of wine.

"He showed up at an investor dinner last week for the winery. He acted really weird all night. Made sure to sit by me, got irritated with Ryan for flirting with me, then…"

"Then?" Emily raises an eyebrow.

"Then he told me he tried to stay away from me, but he can't. He kissed me and invited me back to his hotel room."

"What the hell, Jessica?" Vivien screeches. Emily tries not to spray wine through her lips. I anticipated this sort of reaction. It's why I waited until tonight to tell them instead of calling or texting last weekend. "I didn't go," I say.

I fill them in on the evening. I don't want them to worry too much since I plan on keeping my distance from Luke as much as possible. I don't tell them about all his attempts at contacting me this week. When they ask if I've heard from him since, I simply say that he called a couple of times, but it was all very professional. I adopt a sense of outrage about the entire series of events, so they follow suit, and we conclude that Luke is an egotistical jerk I should definitely stay away from.

The time with them goes by quickly and easily. We decide we should absolutely order a third bottle of wine and Uber home. I quickly check my phone to make sure I don't have missed calls or messages. When I look up, Emily has a Cheshire cat grin plastered on her face.

"Don't turn around, but my future ex-husband is about to walk over here. He's been eyeing our table all night. I'm calling dibs now." Emily looks like she may jump across the table at this poor guy.

She has never been married and doesn't have any real aspirations to. She enjoys dating and her independence. This is my first experience being a single adult, and although I can't say I've been enjoying it, I hope someday I will.

"Well, hello there, handsome," Emily says playfully to the man approaching from behind me.

"Good evening."

His voice is sexy, with just enough gravel in it. Wait a minute, I know that voice.

"Jessica?"

You. Have. Got. To. Be. Kidding. Me.

Luke stands behind me. He appears relaxed and harmless in his jeans and button-up charcoal gray shirt. I know better.

"What are you doing here?" I quickly turn to the table. It doesn't take my friends long to figure out who he is, given my undoubtedly bright red face. Emily grins at me, and Vivien's mouth hangs open.

Luke takes it upon himself to lead introductions. "Hello, I'm Luke Taylor. Jessica and I know each other from high school and have recently reconnected. In fact, we will be working together."

"That's wonderful," my traitor friend Emily responds. Vivien only nods and politely smiles. "My name is Emily, and this is Vivien."

"Nice to meet you Emily and Vivien. Jessica, maybe a dance later?"

"I don't dance." It's not even a good lie. All three of them know I love to dance.

Luke lets out a little laugh. "Maybe you will change your mind after you lovely ladies finish your bottle of wine. Enjoy your evening."

As Luke walks away, I take a big gulp of my wine. Then I take another.

"Holy shit," Vivien whispers, and I can hear the concern in her voice.

"I changed my mind, Jessica. You do not need to stay away from that man. You need to have wild, crazy, life-changing sex with him." Emily sounds serious, but I've drunk a lot of wine, so I'm not sure.

"Emily!" Vivien shrieks at her. I sit silent, an observer to the conversation. It reminds me of one of those out-of-body experiences people talk about.

"Don't 'Emily' me! Did you see him?" Emily practically shouts at Vivien. "Did you notice the way he was staring at her? He's been watching our table for the past hour." She pauses, and I envision cogs working in her head. "He wants her. Bad. He's exactly the right kind of man to help you get over an asshole ex-husband with no bedroom skills."

I can't suppress a giggle. I made the mistake of drinking a little too much one night after finding out about Grant's affair. I didn't go into detail, but I did say he hadn't given me an orgasm in years.

"He seems like trouble to me, and before you say it, Emily, not the good kind."

I can always depend on Vivien to be level-headed.

"Maybe. He may be worth it. I'm not saying marry the guy, but maybe enjoy what he has to offer." Emily ogles Luke from across the room. "And from my vantage point, he has a lot to offer."

"Not everyone thinks like you do." Vivien pinches her lips together. "Some women want more than just a good time."

"Everyone wants to have a good time. Most people simply overthink it."

Emily's eyes are glassy, and I know it's mostly the wine talking at this point. I'm obviously right there with her, because I wonder if what Emily is saying isn't in fact a good idea.

"We already established that her getting involved with him again was potentially a very bad idea. You can't change your mind because he happens to be attractive."

"Oh yes I can. I was expecting attractive. I was not expecting that." Emily waves in Luke's direction. I don't look. "Maybe we have underestimated our dear friend Jessica. Maybe she can engage in meaningless, hot, sweaty—"

"Stay on topic, Emily," Vivien says and sighs.

"I'm only saying, if she wants to let that beautiful man over there take her home one night, that would be okay, and we should support her."

My friends continue to argue over whether I should or shouldn't use Luke to get over Grant while I finish my wine. It helps to dull the conflict in my brain.

"I'm going to dance," I announce suddenly and get up. The wine decides Emily is right: Luke is hot and I should take advantage of what he's offering. As long as I go in with the idea that it's only for fun and don't allow myself to get emotionally attached, I'll be fine. It will probably even help me move on from Grant more quickly.

This is a great idea. Maybe the best idea I've had in a long time. I confidently approach the corner where Luke is sitting. My view of the table must have been obstructed, because as I get closer, I realize he's not alone. A very pretty blonde is sitting across from him, and they are deep in conversation.

I hear Emily express her disapproval as I pivot and head for the bar instead. A group of men, so young looking I wonder if they are old enough to be here, are taking shots. One of the better-looking ones smiles at me, and my brain jumps to Plan B. I ask him to dance. He sets his drink on the bar, and I lead him out onto the dance floor, where I'm sure Luke will see us.

Luke is still talking with the blonde. He doesn't seem to have noticed my little display yet. He must be saying something hilarious, judging by the way the woman tosses her head back in laughter. I wonder why it feels hot in here all of a sudden.

I don't bother to ask my dance partner's name, because I honestly don't care, nor will I remember it anyway. I move my hips to the music. I don't stop him when he places his hands on my hips and pulls me closer to him. I glance at the corner again. The blonde is still sitting there, but she's on her phone. Luke is scowling at me.

We rotate, and I catch a view of our table. Vivien and Emily express very different reactions. Vivien frowns, and Emily gives me a full smile. I assume their reactions are due to me asking this stranger to dance.

"Excuse me, you need to give us a moment." I whip my head around and come face to face with an angry but restrained Luke. He is obviously talking to my dance partner, but his eyes stay fixed on me.

My young dance partner appears disappointed and clearly unsure what he should do next. His eyes plead for me to tell him whether he should say something or walk away. Luke has presence, and I can tell the guy is intimidated. I consider telling Luke to go away, but it wouldn't be fair to drag this innocent bystander into my drama. I nod slightly, and he hastily retreats back to the bar and his shot-downing friends.

"What are you doing?" Luke rubs the back of his neck, glaring at me.

"Dancing." I try to sound casual, but my voice betrays me and cracks a little. I hate that he's somehow made me feel like I've done something wrong.

"That guy was getting the wrong idea."

"What kind of wrong idea?" I shouldn't poke the bear, but the wine makes me do it.

He shakes his head in frustration, then grips my hips. "That you're interested in him. That he could take you home tonight." He says it so matter-of-factly, it takes me a moment to process. But when I do, I'm livid.

"First of all, maybe I am interested in him." Damn, I wish I'd asked his name now. "Second, dancing does not equal going home with someone. Third, if I want to go home with him, I will. Fourth…" I already can't remember what my fourth point was going to be. I wish I hadn't drunk so much wine.

"Are you done?" Luke crosses his arms. "My turn. First of all, you're not interested in that guy. You don't even know his name.

Second, dancing is fine, but letting a guy grope you because you're trying to make me jealous is not. Third, you will not be going home with anyone tonight. You've had too much to drink, and I won't allow it. Fourth, the woman I'm sitting with is my assistant. She's in town to help me with some paperwork, and we're simply hanging out after a long day of work."

Ah yes, my fourth point was going to be the blonde. I really hate that he's making more sense than I am. I have nothing else to say, so I turn around and head to the table to get my purse.

"I'm leaving," I announce to Vivien and Emily.

"I'll drive her home," Luke says with equal authority as he walks up behind me.

"I'll call an Uber." I dig my phone out of my purse.

Luke grabs it. "Don't be ridiculous. It's late on a Friday night. I don't like the idea of you getting into a stranger's car if you don't have to." He releases a frustrated sigh. "Let me take you home."

I'm tired. I really don't want to wait for a car, but I also don't want to give Luke the satisfaction of doing what he's telling me to.

"I think it's a good idea if you take her home." Vivien elbows Emily for her comment. "An Uber will take at least half an hour. You're ready to go now, he's willing to drive you home—I don't see the downside here."

"See, even your friends know it's a good idea." Luke is pretending to wait for my answer, but I know he's already decided for me.

I'm too worn out to argue, so I mumble something that's a cross between "okay" and "fine."

On our way to the exit, Luke veers off to say something to his assistant, who is still sitting at the table. I contemplate making a run for it but remember I have nowhere to go and I'm in heels. An escape is probably not going to play out well for me. I'm embarrassed by my behavior, but at least now I realize I would not be capable of doing anything with Luke without feelings getting involved. I want to gouge out his assistant's eyes simply for being here with him tonight.

We walk to Luke's car in silence. Once we're seated inside his rental car, he asks for my address. These are the only words we speak the entire drive to my house.

When we arrive, he pulls into the driveway and turns off the engine.

"Well, goodnight." I reach for the door in an attempt to make a quick getaway. My phone beeps, indicating I have a new text message. Always afraid it could be something regarding Amelia, I quickly dig it out of my purse. It's a message from Grant. "Great."

"Everything okay?"

I've never been good at hiding my emotions, and he can tell something's wrong from that one word. If he had any doubt, the tears that are now running down my cheeks and ruining my makeup make it very clear that no, everything is not okay.

"Oh, it's nothing."

"Those are a lot of tears over nothing. Do you want to talk about it?"

I'm a little drunk and a lot tired. I quickly estimate I can be asleep in my bed quicker if I tell Luke about the text instead of trying to give some made-up reason for my tears. "That was Grant. He's bringing his new girlfriend to our daughter's soccer game tomorrow. Should be a great time. Them together, me alone." I squeeze my eyes shut. "I'm sorry, that came out wrong. I'm tired, so I'll just say thank you for the ride home. I'm sure I'll overanalyze all my choices tonight and regret most of them, so I'll apologize now for my drunkenness and bad decisions."

Luke is staring out the windshield when I turn my head toward him. He doesn't say anything and appears to be deep in thought.

I lean my head against the headrest. "We'll be working together, and I want to figure out a way to be around each other without it being so awkward."

"I'm not trying to make this uncomfortable for you." Luke's voice is softer than normal. He opens his mouth to say something, thinks better of it, and closes his mouth. He brushes my hair behind my ear. "Listen, it's late. What I want to say can wait."

I open the door, but he starts speaking again.

"Jessica…"

"Yeah, Luke?"

"I'm sorry he hurt you."

His words cause physical pain in my chest. I get out, but turn back to say one last thing to him before I walk away. "That's ironic coming from you."

His eyes widen and then drop. He allows me the dignity of walking to my doorstep alone, fresh tears rolling down my cheeks.

Chapter 7

My alarm goes off early, too early for a Saturday. The fog takes a minute to lift, but then memories of the previous evening flood in. The text from Grant, the night out with the girls, Luke. As much as I would love to sit in bed and relive every excruciating detail, I don't have time. I need to make myself presentable before I pick up Amelia from Sam's house and get her to the soccer game. My head is pounding, but I'll be damned if I'm going to look awful today. My usual Saturday attire consists of shorts, a T-shirt, and flip-flops. I decide today is the day to wear my new pink floral sundress. Amelia was helping me shop one day and brought it to me. When I saw it on the hanger, I didn't think it was my style, but I felt pretty when I put it on. I could really use some of that confidence today.

I pick up Amelia a few minutes early so we have time to hit our favorite coffee shop. I'm not going to survive today without a major caffeine injection. I order a large coffee instead of my usual chai tea. Amelia wants a drink made primarily of sugar and whipped cream. I usually say no and talk her into something less sugary, but not today.

It dawns on me, as we drive to the sports park, what a breath-takingly beautiful morning it is. The sun is out, and there are a few white puffy clouds in the sky. Skies like this always remind me of preschool. We would lay on the playground, staring up at the clouds and giggling about the shapes we would see. Eventually someone would blurt out something inappropriate, and the activity would be over as our teacher redirected our attention to something else. I was a serious little girl and was always upset when someone else had to ruin a good thing with their foolishness. Adult life isn't that much different than preschool.

My daydream is interrupted by Amelia raising her voice to sing the chorus of Adele's "Someone Like You." She is a car singer, like her mommy, but definitely more talented. I join in with her, focusing on the lyrics. Even though I was happily married when this song first came out, something about it always made me think of Luke. Now it makes me think of Luke and Grant.

The song is over, and the radio station cuts to commercial. I think about Grant's message from last night. The pain has dulled after a good cry and some sleep, but it still hurts. Today is Amelia's first soccer game of the season, and I will not let us ruin it. I'm determined to show up at that game, looking amazing, with a fake smile plastered on my face to prove to everyone how great I'm doing.

I don't see Grant's car in the parking lot when we arrive. Maybe God has heard my prayers. I don't wish anyone harm, but a minor accident or case of food poisoning preventing their arrival would be welcome.

As soon as we're parked, Amelia takes off, dribbling toward where her team has assembled to run warm-up drills. I'm grabbing my bag and chair from the back of my SUV when I'm startled by a familiar voice.

"Good morning, Jessica."

"Good morning, Grant." I muster as much cheerfulness as I can. He seems well, so apparently vomiting was not part of his morning.

"This is Stephanie, my…" Grant stumbles over his words as the woman next to him steps forward to shake my hand. At least Grant has the decency to appear uncomfortable.

"Nice to meet you," I say, so I don't have to hear him say the actual word. Stephanie is not the name on the texts I found on his phone. She must be new. She is pretty, almost too pretty. She obviously spends a lot of time and money to look the way she does. Highlighted hair, manicured nails, perfectly coordinated outfit. It's not fair how women judge each other. If someone shows up in sweats and no makeup, we assume she has let herself go or there must be something wrong with her. If she shows up well put-together, then she must be vain. Men aren't as hard on each other. You would never hear a man belittle another man because of his decision to not shave that day. "The game is about to start. We better get down there."

We walk to the field in silence, but I make sure to have a smile on my face. I don't know exactly what I'm trying to accomplish or prove, but ever since I was a kid, I've had this desire to make everyone else comfortable. If I pretend I'm okay going to my daughter's soccer game with my soon-to-be ex-husband and his new girlfriend, then the situation will be less uncomfortable for everyone. I don't want others to know my heart is being juiced like an orange while it's still inside me. If they knew, they would look at me with pity in their eyes.

I say good morning to the other parents as I set up my chair. I pretend I'm searching for something in my bag as

Grant introduces Stephanie to everyone. I make sure to smile at everyone who makes eye contact with me. My coping strategy is making me feel like a complete fraud.

At halftime, Amelia comes over to get a snack and give hugs to everyone. I'm caught off guard when she hugs Stephanie too. I clench my jaw so tight, I worry about cracking my teeth. I calm myself down by rationalizing that Amelia has always been very friendly. I remember the time I had to stop her from hugging a stranger at the store after she complemented Amelia's dress. I have nearly convinced myself that her affectionate gesture means next to nothing when I notice a man approaching our field. Even from a distance, I can tell he's tall, with muscular arms. He has a baseball cap and sunglasses on and is carrying a beach chair over his shoulder. I don't recognize him until he gets closer, then I let out a tiny gasp.

"Hey, sorry I'm late. Do you mind if I squeeze my chair in right here?" Luke addresses me and the mom sitting next to me. She silently nods and scoots over. By the way she's staring at Luke, I don't think she minds trading our opportunity to chat for a chance to sit next to him for the remainder of the game. Luke squeezes my forearm as he takes his seat and turns his attention to the field, where the game is about to resume.

"What are you doing here?" I smile as I whisper, trying to make this situation appear a lot more natural than it is. I also do not want to draw any more attention to us, though it doesn't matter. People are already watching us.

"You're welcome." He keeps his eyes on the game.

"I don't understand why you're here. Did you follow me?" I ask, trying to remember if I did in fact invite him last night in my drunkenness.

"I thought you could use some help." He shrugs off my question, like him being here makes complete sense.

"Help? With what?"

"I knew today was going to be hard for you, so I thought I could help. Is your daughter number ten? She's pretty good."

"I don't need your help!" I blurt out like a five-year-old after being told she is too small to pour her own juice. I quickly replace the scowl on my face with a smile and lower my voice. "He's my ex-husband. I can handle him on my own."

"He's not the one you need saving from." Luke is still focused on the game.

"From her then?" My voice strains as I try to contain my outrage. "I'm not in competition with her." As much as I want them to be true, my words don't ring true even to me.

"Not from her either." Luke sighs. "From yourself. Sometimes you need to be saved from yourself. You need to let him go."

I want to be anywhere but here. This day is turning out to be more than I can handle. It's bad enough dealing with Grant and Stephanie, but I have to contend with Luke too. How dare he come here uninvited and try to give me relationship advice. But I won't make a scene, so all I can do is stare at the soccer game and pray it doesn't go into overtime.

This prayer is answered. The game is over, and I frantically gather my belongings. I audibly gasp when Grant walks over to introduce himself to Luke.

"Jessica, we wanted to say goodbye." I hate that he's already using "we" when talking about himself and this other woman. "It was nice to see you." Grant addresses me more like an acquaintance than the woman he was married to for almost eight years. "Are you going to introduce us to your friend?"

"Luke Taylor." Luke introduces himself, because I have lost the ability to form words. Grant pales, and I know it's because he's just remembered where he knows Luke from. Although Grant has never officially met Luke, he knows all about him and our past.

"Oh, well, nice to meet you. I'm Jessica's husband, Grant."

"Husband? I guess, technically, but not for long." Luke focuses on Grant unapologetically.

"I mean, yes, we're separated." Grant is visibly shaken by Luke's directness.

"Not only separated, getting divorced." Luke is not going to let Grant off the hook.

"The process takes a long time." Grant's hesitation is because he doesn't want to concede to Luke, but with Stephanie eagerly listening, he is forced to, at least partially.

Luke eyes Grant but decides his point has been made. He offers a hand to Stephanie and flashes her a smile. "Hi. I'm Luke."

"Stephanie." Even with Grant standing here, she is gawking at Luke.

Luke returns his attention to Grant and studies him a moment. "It's great to finally meet you both. Being able to attend your daughter's events together is important. I'm glad everyone is ready to move on." Grant flinches, and Luke capitalizes on his upper hand. "You can imagine how difficult and awkward it would be if you were uncomfortable with how quickly Jessica has moved on." Luke laughs lightly to break the tension he has created. "I'm glad we can all be mature about this."

I'm about to pray for an earthquake when Amelia runs in to save the day.

"There's my girl. Great game!" I exclaim a little too enthusiastically. "Oh wow, it's already eleven o'clock. We really need to get going."

Everyone congratulates Amelia on her game, politely shakes hands, and says their goodbyes. After we finish lying about how nice it was to meet each other, I hurry toward my car.

"Jessica, wait." Luke is far enough off that I can get away with pretending not to hear him.

I'm already replaying the events of the morning in my head while trying to get to my car quickly and avoid twisting my ankle. Why did I wear this dress and wedge sandals? I remember telling myself while I was getting ready this morning that I am not in competition with Grant's new girlfriend. A realization hits me like a truck. I'm not in competition with her because she's already won. Everyone else can see my relationship with Grant is over. Even Luke sees it. I got dressed up to impress who today? A man who no longer looks at me? A woman I don't even know? I even had another man show up to make him jealous. Even though I didn't plan that, everyone will think it. How pathetic I must seem. This must be what Luke meant by saving me from myself.

I throw open the back of my SUV and toss our stuff in with shaky hands. Approaching footsteps alert me I wasn't fast enough. Luke is going to catch up with me before I can complete my getaway.

I glance up at Luke and imagine I look like a bunny caught in a trap. He makes sure Amelia is inside before speaking. "Jessica, he doesn't want you—"

"You think I don't know that?" I yell without a shred of composure. "You think I don't remember that every single day?"

I close my eyes and clear my throat before continuing in a calmer manner. "I get it, okay? I'm the dull old wife, jealous of the shiny new girlfriend. Damn it, you'd think I'd be used to being replaced by now." I'm referring to our past as much as I am my crumbled marriage, and he knows it. He flinches, and part of me likes that I've caused him discomfort. I'm careful not to think of it as pain, because I'm not sure Luke Taylor is capable of feeling that. He's like Grant; they take what they want for as long as they can, and then they leave.

Luke looks like he's going to say something else, but I've had enough.

"Stop. I've sufficiently embarrassed myself, it's time to call it a day." I don't need to explain myself to him, but my over-active brain won't let me walk away without finishing my thought. "I may have looked foolish today, but I was a good wife and a good mom, and I deserved better." I turn on my heeled sandals and escape into the SUV.

Amelia is already engrossed in a game on her tablet. I quickly back out of the parking space and flee. I can't help but take one last glimpse in my rearview mirror. Luke's standing where I left him, shoulders slumped, head hanging.

Chapter 8

I spend the rest of the weekend trying to distract myself, with varying levels of success. The time I spend with Amelia baking cookies is a happy distraction. It's slightly chaotic every time she helps me in the kitchen. The counters and floors wind up covered in a white dusting of flour and sugar. The messiness makes me cringe, but she is so full of joy while she is doing it that I work hard to let go. I remind myself to focus on the fun and not the disastrous condition of my kitchen.

When Monday morning arrives, I'm still angry about the soccer game on Saturday—angry at Grant for being insensitive and putting me in an uncomfortable situation, furious at Luke for his unsolicited help. Luke reminding me that Grant doesn't want me anymore was particularly cruel.

I arrive at the winery and spend the first fifteen minutes chatting with Linda. I tell her about my night out with the girls and my run-in with Grant and his new girlfriend, although I omit the detail about Luke showing up at both places. Linda tells me she had dinner at the new restaurant downtown and wasn't impressed. After our weekend recaps, I sit at my desk and start my week. My work phone is blinking, indicating I have a new message. I dial my voicemail and frown when a familiar voice greets me. It's Luke. He asks why I didn't return any of his calls on Saturday or Sunday. I delete the message and get started answering emails. I let all outside incoming calls go directly to voicemail. At the end of the day, I sort through them. Out of six, five are from Luke. His messages get increasingly shorter. In the final message of the day, he simply states that we need to talk. I don't respond.

Tuesday morning begins with texts from Luke. I begin to read the first one but only get through "Please call me, we need to talk about..." before I delete it. I spend part of my day deleting all additional texts from him without opening them. If it's something business related, Aaron will contact me.

The next morning starts with more promise. I receive no texts and am relieved to find no messages waiting for me when I arrive at work. The day is productive, and I'm getting a lot accomplished in a short amount of time. In between reviewing legal documents Mrs. Bianchi requested I look over, I overhear Linda thank our delivery woman, Maggie.

"They're beautiful," Maggie says before walking out and shutting the door.

My curiosity is piqued, so I leave my desk to see what's going on. I assume Linda has received flowers again. Her husband sends them to her from time to time, sometimes for no particular reason. Every time she gets a new delivery, I experience a pinch of jealousy. I haven't received flowers in years. Grant thought they were a waste of money. He didn't want to spend money on something that was just going to die.

Perched on Linda's desk is a large fragrant vase of star-gazer lilies.

"They're for you." Linda wears a wide grin.

I tentatively open the card, unable to help a laugh. As punishment for my envy, I discover the flowers are from Luke.

"So…who are they from?"

"They're a thank-you from one of our investors." I don't like to lie to Linda, so I go with a half-truth.

"That was thoughtful. Quite a coincidence that they knew what your favorite type of flower is." Linda gives me a knowing smile.

"Yes, well, I have to get back to work." I hurry back to my office, cheeks flushed.

I remind myself who I'm dealing with. I refuse to be won over because Luke happens to remember what my favorite flower is.

An hour later, I hear Maggie talking to Linda again. Linda doesn't say anything when she sets the bouquet of orange roses on my desk next to the stargazers. My lack of eye contact confirms her suspicions that these are not more thank-you flowers.

Three more arrangements arrive before lunch. Before leaving to get something to eat, I ask Linda to pass them along to other departments. By the time I return from picking up my smoothie, my desk is mostly clear. Linda has left the stargazers and a small stack of cards on my desk. I pick up the stack and put them in my purse.

Linda pokes her head in. "You received two more bouquets. I don't know who they're from, but I left the cards on your desk. I hope you don't mind, but I left the stargazers too. Figured you'd want to keep such a beautiful thank-you gift." Linda returns to her desk without waiting for a response.

Later, after Amelia is tucked into bed, my curiosity gets the better of me. I open all the cards and lay them across my kitchen island. Luke's handwriting swirls across them.

Waiting for you to remember how good we are together.

We've spent too much time assuming things. We need to talk and figure us out.

You're not mine to think about, but I do anyway.

Your voice is my favorite sound, and my ears haven't heard it for too long.

I've wasted too much of my life missing you, when I should have been with you.

I keep thinking about our kiss at the investor dinner. It's time to make up for all the years I should have been kissing you.

Maybe I don't deserve you, but I would like to become the kind of man who does.

His words are more poignant than I anticipated. I shouldn't have read the cards. Luke invades my dreams more than once as I try to sleep.

I wake up exhausted in the morning. Despite my tiredness, I'm prepared for whatever new tactic Luke is planning for today. When lunch is delivered, I'm not overly surprised. In another attempt by Luke to get my attention, Mexican food has been provided for all the administrative staff, compliments of our new investors. The fact that it's from my favorite restaurant is probably not a coincidence. I'm still disturbed by him knowing where to show up the last couple of times I've seen him. As puzzling as it is, I have no intention of ever getting the opportunity to ask him about it.

Luke is the type of man who is used to getting what he wants. I'm not foolish enough to let him hurt me again. If I ignore him, he will eventually find someone else to pursue. It's obvious by the way women react to him and the way he carries himself that he has been thoroughly enjoying his single life. The life he craved when he broke up with me. At some point he will tire of the chase, move on, and forget about me once again. I need to stay away from him until that happens because I don't always have a clear head about what's best for me when he's near.

Luke leaves one more voicemail Friday morning, but all messages and deliveries have stopped by Friday afternoon. I congratulate myself on being strong enough to resist the charms of Luke Taylor. Linda called out sick, and after a long meeting discussing new software implementation, I get ready to head home a little early. It's Grant's weekend with Amelia, and I'll be spending the weekend alone. I asked my mom earlier in the week if she wanted to have dinner, but she reminded me this is the weekend she's traveling to Florida to see my aunt Susie.

I pick up the phone to call Vivien.

"Hey Jess," she answers after one ring.

"Hey there. I know it's last minute, but what are you up to tonight?"

"Eddie and I are going to dinner and a movie. You're welcome to join us."

Her invitation is sincere, and I have joined them before, but I don't feel like being the third wheel tonight. "Thanks, but I'll pass this time. You two enjoy your evening together."

"Are you sure? We'd love for you to come."

"Yeah, thanks for the offer though. Tell Eddie I said hi."

"Okay. Call you tomorrow?"

"Sounds good." I hang up and dial Emily next.

"Hi sexy lady."

"Em, what are you doing tonight?"

"Actually, I have a date."

"Oh yeah? Who's the lucky guy?"

"Someone I met at the gym. He's Luke Taylor hot." She must be in a playful mood, because she laughs at her comment, a comment she knows will annoy me.

"Okay, that cannot be your new phrase."

"Fine, he's Hemsworth hot."

"Which one?"

"Does it matter?" We both laugh.

"How did you meet this guy?" I'm eager to hear. Emily often has amusing stories about her dating life.

"He got on the stair climber next to me as I was about to get off. Needless to say, I stayed on for another thirty minutes, talking to him."

"Did you ask him out or did he ask you?" Emily tends to be aggressive with men. We've tried to suggest she let them come to her, but she rarely listens.

"He asked me out," she says hesitantly.

"Emily, what did you say to him?"

"Nothing. I just told him that since he already made me hot and sweaty at our first meeting, I couldn't wait to see what our first date would be like."

"Emily!"

"Jessica!" Emily mocks my tone and laughs.

"I give up." I shake my head even though she can't see me. "I just talked to Vivien, and she invited me to dinner with her and Ed. Aren't you going to invite me to join you tonight?"

"Are you asking to have a threesome with me and the hot gym guy?" Emily teases.

"Absolutely not. I was simply pointing out that Vivien is a better friend than you," I tease back.

"Vivien has sex more regularly than either of us. That's why she's nicer. Consider me going on this date my attempt to be a better friend." "Wow, it's going to have to be some amazing sex for that to happen."

"I think he's up for it."

"You're awful. Have fun tonight and be safe."

"Thanks. I'll talk to you later."

I hang up, turn off my computer, and gather my belongings.

I'm not terribly disappointed everyone had other things to do tonight. I could use the quiet. My original plans involving a new romance novel I downloaded to my Kindle and a hot bath will remain intact.

"Good night, Albert." I wave to one of the maintenance guys. "Have a great weekend." I always feel guilty saying that, knowing that his position will require him to work all weekend.

I'm distracted as I walk to my car, mentally deliberating dinner options while trying to locate the keys in my purse. When I look up, I notice a limo parked directly behind my car.

"Great," I mutter. It probably recently delivered someone who is getting married on the property tonight. I hope the driver is still inside so he can move the vehicle. I'm already brainstorming an alternative plan to get out of the parking lot when the driver gets out and walks to the back passenger door.

"Excuse me?" He doesn't respond, so I assume he hasn't heard me. I smile when he opens the door, waiting for a bride or groom to emerge from the limo.

My smile disappears when I see it's not a member of the bridal party. It's Luke.

Maybe I shouldn't be, but I'm surprised. I open my mouth, but he raises his hand before I have a chance to say anything.

"We need to talk. Get in." His words are short and sharp but not angry.

"No thank you." I alter my path to walk around the back of the limo.

Luke steps aside enough to remain in front of me. "You can make this more difficult if you want, but you will end up talking to me. I'm known to be very persistent, and I will come back here as often as I need to until you have a conversation with me." The serious expression on his face makes me believe every word he says.

I still don't want to talk to him though. "That's called harassment. I don't think there's anything left to—"

"As often as I need to," Luke says. Him running a hand through his hair reminds me of a younger Luke…less sure of himself, less in control. "Please, one conversation."

I nod. I know him well enough to know he's not bluffing. I move to the door of the limo.

He motions for me to enter first. I slide in and scoot all the way to the other side. He gets in after me. When he notices where I've chosen to sit, he smirks.

"Drive," he says to the driver, who has returned to the front seat.

"I'm not going anywhere with you. This is only going to be a quick conversation." I try not to panic.

"Yes, it'll be quick. I don't want to block others in the parking lot."

The driver rolls up the partition, and I'm effectively confined in a small space with Luke. I'm more nervous than I'd like to admit but determined not to show it. I imagine I'm in a business negotiation.

I busy myself digging my phone from my purse. I feel his eyes on me, like he's studying me, trying to read me. When I raise my gaze to meet his, he closes his eyes and tilts his head back. I don't want to misread the situation, but he almost seems nervous. I'm not sure I've ever seen Luke this uneasy. He takes a deep breath and runs a hand through his hair again. I wonder if his hair is as soft as I remember.

"You're upset about what happened at the soccer game, about what I said." He pauses and looks directly at me. "I said you need to let him go, because you do. But not for the reasons you're thinking. You need to let him go not because he's moved on, but because you deserve better."

"Of course I do." At least we can agree on something.

"I'm serious. You deserve someone who values you."

"I couldn't agree more." Does he realize he's fueling my reasons to stay away from him?

"I also said he didn't want you."

The words make my heart sink as far down into my stomach as they did the first time he said them. "If you came here to recap what you said to me last weekend, there's no need. I remember." My delivery is sharp, and Luke flinches.

"I regret that my words sounded harsh, but I didn't get to finish my thought." He sighs. "I was going to say that he doesn't want you…the way I want you."

His words make my heart ache in an entirely different way this time. I hate that he affects me so easily, but I maintain my resolve. "What you're offering isn't something I'm interested in."

"What do you think I'm offering?"

"Sex." My forwardness shocks me as much as it does him.

He nods. "Don't get me wrong, that would be great, but I apologize if I gave you the impression that's all I'm interested in. I could never just have sex with you anymore than you could with me." He leans toward me. "I meant every word I wrote on those cards."

"I didn't read all of them." I fidget with the hem of my blazer.

"You're not very good at that, you know." Luke leans back against the seat.

"What?"

He smiles. "Lying."

I don't think discussing the words he wrote is in my best interest. His charm can be distracting, so I change the subject.

"Okay, so if not just sex, why in the world would you think I'd put myself in a position to be hurt by you again?" The words are honest, and they feel powerful coming out of my mouth.

"Good. This is what we really need to talk about." Luke rests his elbows on his knees. "We never discussed what happened between us. As much as neither of us is looking forward to this conversation, we need to have it."

"Actually, we don't. I know what happened. You graduated and left." I bite down on my lip, hoping the pain there will somehow lessen the pain in my heart. It doesn't.

"It's time we laid it all out." Luke watches me earnestly.

"Fine." I take a deep breath. "I loved you, and you left. You left, and it felt like the years we were together didn't matter, like they weren't real. I don't know, maybe they weren't real for you, but they were for me." Tears collect in my eyes.

"Of course they were real. My feelings for you always have been." He looks at me, then away. "Fuck, this is harder than I thought. Truth? I was an eighteen-year-old kid, away from home for the first time. People kept telling me I was making a mistake being tied down to a girlfriend thousands of miles away. I was playing on one of the best college baseball teams in the country and getting a lot of attention from everyone." His lips tighten. "I started believing my own hype. I talked myself into believing that breaking up would be best for both of us. That we got together too young and we needed to go out, experience other things. Other people." He shakes his head and closes his eyes. "Hearing you break down on the phone that night, the night I ended things…" He pauses. "I felt like shit after we hung up, but I was still convinced I was doing the right thing."

I'm not surprised by Luke's reasons for breaking up with me. That much I figured out on my own. I am surprised by his admission of how the breakup affected him. My recollection of that evening is of me crying and him repeating, "This will be better for both of us." At the time, I interpreted it as him not really caring and trying to minimize my reaction.

"I admit the first few weeks were kind of fun. I was able to flirt and not feel guilty about it, but I wasn't happy. I felt like a loser for missing you so much, so I pretended I didn't. By the time I came home for Christmas break, I knew what I needed to do. I was going to ride into town, beg for your forgiveness, and we'd pick back up where we left off." He gazes at the limo's ceiling. "I was so cocky, it never even crossed my mind that my plan wouldn't work."

I remember that Christmas break. It was my senior year, and I'd spent the majority of the first semester moping around and listening to sad breakup songs. Karen was growing tired of my depression and insisted we go to a party that one of the guys on the football team was throwing. I didn't want to go, but I felt like I owed it to her for being such a crappy friend. I met Grant at that party.

"Matt was home from college too. When I told him my plan, he said we should go to a party a friend of his younger brother was throwing, that maybe you'd be there. When I arrived, the place was packed. It took me a while, but I finally found you. You were sitting at a table in the backyard with Karen and some people I didn't know. You were stunning in a red V-neck sweater, and you were smiling. No, not simply smiling—glowing." Luke lets out a long sigh. "I don't know what I expected, but I was surprised to see you so happy. A guy sat down next to you and handed you a drink. You looked at him, and in that instant I knew. You looked at him the way you looked at me the first time we met. I realized in that moment I was watching you love someone else." Luke's eyes contain a sadness that wasn't there before.

My heart squeezes in my chest. I had instant chemistry with Grant. I hadn't wanted to go to the party, but once I was there, I felt like it was destiny. Grant was from out of town, visiting his cousin. He was clearly interested in me. He was attentive and expressive of how he felt about me, two things I was desperately craving. The memory of Grant and me is as painful as the realization that Luke witnessed it.

"It was the worst night of my life up until that point. I made Matt promise never to say anything to anyone, especially you. I know it isn't fair, but I was so angry at you for picking him. I really believed you were supposed to be with me, and I blamed you for not knowing it too." Luke isn't looking at me anymore, like it pains him to do so. "Matt would hear things and keep me updated on the status of your relationship. The new worst night of my life occurred when Matt called to tell me he heard you were engaged. I decided then I would never allow someone to get close enough to hurt me. Or to be hurt by me."

Even though I did nothing wrong with Grant, knowing Luke's side explains some things. "Luke, I don't know what to say. You can't be mad at me for moving on after you broke up with me."

Luke shakes his head. "I know. I didn't handle any of it how I should have. I thought my feelings had dulled over the years, until I saw you at the reunion. I honestly didn't think you'd be there. I got hopeful when I spotted you standing there alone. Then I saw your wedding ring, and the anger I felt years ago came roaring back to life. I watched you and couldn't figure out why you looked sad even when you were laughing. Then I heard you were getting a divorce. I hated to see you pretending to be all right when I could see you weren't. I was still angry, but not with you."

"Please don't…I can't…" My eyes refill with tears, but this time I'm unable to keep them from spilling over. I wipe my cheeks.

"I was mad at myself. Mad at the thought that I may have caused you to look or act like that at one point." Luke slides over next to me, but he doesn't touch me. "I understand why you don't want to discuss anything about your divorce with me. I hate that you have to go through this, but I have to admit, I wonder if things didn't work out with Grant because you're supposed to be with me."

"Luke…I don't know what you're expecting me to say." I repeat the same words for a second time in the last few minutes.

"I don't have any expectations. I'm sure we will need to revisit this subject again at some point, but I wanted you to know my side." He reaches up and wipes my cheek. "We both could use a break from this topic, which brings me to the other subject I came to talk to you about. I have to attend a charity dinner tonight in San Francisco, and I want you to come with me."

His invitation startles me. I swipe under my eyes in case any mascara has run. I glance around as the car comes to a stop. We're in the parking lot of the French Valley Airport. It's a small local airport, used primarily for private planes. "Right now? I can't go with you right now."

"Why?"

"I'm a mother. I have responsibilities." I assume Luke is unfamiliar with the constraints of being a parent. I'm sure he can hop on a plane and go anywhere at a moment's notice, but I can't.

"Do you have Amelia this weekend?"

"Well, no." I try to come up with another excuse. "I haven't packed anything."

"My assistant has already made arrangements to have everything you might need waiting for you when we arrive."

"How could she…how would she…you don't even know what size I wear."

"I can accurately guess what size you wear." Luke smirks at me.

The implication that he has examined me closely enough to determine my size makes heat rise in my cheeks.

"Listen, no pressure, no expectations. I would simply like to spend some time with you."

I rack my brain for another reason why I can't go. *I don't trust myself around you* would be the honest answer, but I know he would get too much enjoyment out of that response, so I remain silent.

Suddenly Luke's lips are pressed against mine. It's unexpected but surprisingly welcome. My hands automatically go up into the hair I've been longing to touch. It is as soft as I remember. The driver knocks on the limo window to let us know it's time to board the plane and Luke slowly pulls his lips away from mine.

"I thought you said no expectations?" I say.

"I don't have any, but that doesn't mean I won't go after what I want this time." Luke flashes me what can only be described as a devilish grin.

Chapter 9

The flight to San Francisco is short and pleasant. I've never been in a private plane before and quickly understand why people who can afford it choose this method of travel. A flight attendant offers to bring us whatever we would like. I ask for iced tea. Luke asks for bottled water. He returns with our drinks, along with slippers and blankets. Luke apologizes for having to answer business emails, but I don't mind. The quiet gives me time to collect my thoughts.

I'm obviously attracted to Luke, but I'm still hesitant about him and where this has the potential to go. If it were anyone else, I wouldn't be worried about the future on a "first date," but then again I wouldn't be on a plane heading out of town either. Nothing about this situation is ordinary, and that makes it difficult for me to know how I should handle it.

I'm deep in thought—or doubt to be more accurate—when Luke finishes typing his last response. He quietly sits next to me and waits for me to speak.

"I'm not sure this was a good idea," I say after a few minutes.

"Remember, no expectations." His expression is soft. I appreciate that he's trying to make me more relaxed, however impossible that may be. "How about we agree not to try to figure anything out tonight? I get to go to a nice dinner with a beautiful woman. It really is that simple."

I nod and sincerely hope he's correct.

A car picks us up at the airport to take us to Luke's home. He assures me I will have my own bedroom on the other side of the residence. I'm curious to see where he lives, seeing as we just stepped off a private plane. He takes a business call during the drive, so I don't get a chance to ask him about it.

We pull up outside a sleek, modern building made of twisting metal and glass. It's not what I envisioned when he said we would be staying at his home.

"Thanks Dean," Luke says to the driver once we're standing on the sidewalk.

I follow Luke through the large glass doors.

The lobby is primarily adorned with white marble and muted gray textured walls. A free-form chandelier hangs from a high ceiling, somehow adding something to the space even though it doesn't particularly stand out. Although I would never describe it as homey, the space manages to convey comfort and simple elegance. We ride the elevator in silence up to the thirtieth floor.

We step into another simply decorated lobby, although much smaller than the one downstairs. He unlocks and enters one of the two doors that have 30A on them. We walk down a short hallway, then the apartment opens into an open plan kitchen, dining room, and living room. Floor-to-ceiling glass windows and doors offer a stunning view of city lights and a bridge. It's mesmerizing.

"It's the Bay Bridge." He's appreciating the view too.

"I know. My mom brought me here once as a little kid. I remember my excitement when she said we could drive across not one, but two big bridges. I'm not sure why I remember that."

"Maybe it means you were meant to come back here someday."

"Maybe."

Luke gives me a mini tour. I'm glad he does, because his apartment is larger than my house, and I'm not sure I would have been able to find my room on my own. The interior is modern, stylish, and very clean. There is a large open living area with leather couches, glass tables, and a fireplace with a glass tile surround. To the right, the kitchen is an impressive display of dark gray cabinets, white marble, and stainless-steel appliances. I'm still trying to take it all in when I realize that I've fallen behind. I follow his voice to another hallway on the other side of the apartment. Luke points out a bathroom and his office before showing me to the guestroom. It is beautifully decorated in varying shades of gray, black, and white. Red accents give it a touch of color. Someone once told me red makes them think of anger, but it always reminds me of love and passion. I wonder what emotions it evokes in him?

"My suite is on the other side of the apartment."

"Okay."

"I'll show you where it is later, so you can sneak in if you want."

"I'll try to control myself." I roll my eyes.

"You'll try." Luke smiles and changes the subject. "Can you be ready in an hour?"

"No problem."

"Great. My assistant should have prepared your room and left everything you need, but let me know if I can get you anything else." He leaves me to get ready.

I had not thought too much about it before today, but between the plane and this apartment, I'm struck with the realization that Luke has money, and a lot of it. It doesn't matter to me one way or another, but it does make me proud of him and what he's obviously been able to accomplish.

As promised, clothes are in the closet, and a variety of feminine toiletries have been placed in the en suite bathroom. I'm not surprised to see the sizes are correct.

I select a plum silk dress, though I should probably call it a gown. The price tag is still attached, indicating it cost more than anything I own, including my designer wedding dress from many years ago. I don't feel entirely comfortable wearing it, but I did agree to come. At this point it would be rude to refuse the dress and not go to the dinner. I select a pair of nude heels, but I don't touch any of the jewelry laid out on top of one of the dressers. The diamond studs I wore to work today will have to do.

Luke is concentrating on something on his phone when I step into the living room. It gives me a moment to appreciate the sight. He is wearing a tuxedo, and he has the perfect build for it. He truly is a striking man.

Luke senses my presence and looks up. He doesn't say anything. He simply stares at me. It's a definite bolster to my confidence that I appear to have rendered Luke Taylor speechless. He makes me feel beautiful and appreciated but self-conscious too.

"Ready?" I break the silence.

"Yeah." Luke's voice is low and throaty. "But if having people look at you makes you uncomfortable, you definitely chose the wrong dress."

I answer a couple of work emails during the short ride to the hotel while Luke does the same. The distraction prevents me from overthinking the fact that I'm going on my first date with him in more than a decade.

We step into the ballroom as they begin to serve dinner, and I follow Luke to a table. Aaron and a pretty redhead are already sitting there. It dawns on me that I work with these men, and showing up with Luke does not appear very professional, especially since Aaron still assumes we only met a few months ago. As if reading my mind, Luke whispers in my ear, "I told Aaron about us after the harvest event."

Aaron and his date stand, and Luke shakes his hand and gives his date a hug.

"Hi, Jessica. We hoped you'd be here tonight. Nice to see you." Aaron hugs me briefly. "This is my wife, Andi."

Andi embraces me too. "I've heard so much about you. So nice to finally meet you."

"Same here." Her welcome is warm and sincere. I instantly like her.

We engage in the typical get-to-know-you talk over dinner. Andi owns her own marketing firm. She and Aaron have been married for ten years and have no children. Apparently, they tried for years at the beginning of their relationship, but it never happened. They decided not to do any fertility testing or treatments and to simply let nature take its course.

After dessert and coffee are served, an elegant gray-haired woman steps up to the podium. She introduces herself as the CEO of the organization. Everything happened so quickly this afternoon, I forgot to ask Luke anything about the dinner or the charity. I learn that the organization is named Second Chances, and they work to provide guidance to and opportunities for troubled youth. When she is done with her opening remarks, she begins a video presentation. It features a young man who grew up in one of the rougher areas of town. He started smoking marijuana at age eleven and was experimenting with harder drugs by thirteen. His mother tried to get him to change his ways, but he wouldn't listen. She reached out to Second Chances and got him enrolled in some of their after-school classes. The opportunity led to the young man discovering a love of cooking. The video concludes with his announcement that, due to the support of the organization, he is currently attending his first year of culinary school.

The video is heartfelt and inspiring. I'm not at all embarrassed that a few tears have rolled down my cheek. I'm already mentally calculating how much I can afford to donate while the audience is still clapping.

The CEO is visibly emotional as she explains how she began the charity after seeing her son struggle to find himself as a young man. She calls up a few board members before beginning the finale of her speech.

"This organization has always depended on the community for support. We have been fortunate over the years, receiving help in the form of time, expertise, and money from numerous members of our community. The need is great and ongoing. This year is no exception. We're asking you all to help as much as you can, to ensure these children have options."

The room erupts into applause again and she waits until it dies down before continuing. "We also wanted to take a moment this evening to introduce our newest board member. He has donated his time, money, and heart in numerous ways over the last four years. When I asked him if he would join our board, he said yes without hesitation. I know he is going to be a valuable addition, as he has exciting ideas on how to grow this organization. It is my pleasure to welcome our newest board member, Luke Taylor."

The room erupts in applause as Luke stands. He approaches the front of the room, where he shakes hands with the other board members. He looks uncharacteristically humble as he steps up to the microphone.

"Thank you, Maggie. Thank you, board. Thanks for this opportunity to make a difference, because that's what we're doing here. I want to share with you the story about how I got involved with this organization. About four years ago, I moved to San Francisco for my job. I found early success in business and was already successful by many measures. I had a fancy apartment. I had a nice car. Honestly, I thought I was pretty hot stuff." Someone in the audience whistles, and everyone, including Luke, laughs.

"I was living a very fortunate life, working hard and making a name for myself in the financial world, but that was all I cared about. I had become a different person, a selfish person. I was lucky enough to have some good people around me though, and they suggested I search for more. My friend

Aaron, who is also my business partner, suggested I volunteer with him at Second Chances one weekend. I thought it was going to be a waste of time. I mean, what did I possibly have to offer these kids? I only went with the sole purpose of getting him off my back for a while." I glance over at Aaron, who is wearing a proud grin. Aaron can't be more than a few years older than Luke, but now I see he has been a sort of mentor to him.

"I never imagined how much that weekend would change me. I was at the center for about an hour, kind of going through the motions, when I met Teddy. Teddy was a twelve-year-old kid, and when I say kid, I mean it. He was sweet and naïve. His older stepbrother had fallen in with a rough crowd, and his mom was scared Teddy might get dragged into it as well. I remember thinking his mom was probably overreacting and there was no way this kid was gang-member material. I spent some time with Teddy, then his mom came to pick him up. I said goodbye and finished my day hanging out with a few of the other kids. That night I went home and figured I had done my good deed for the year." Luke pauses, the weight of a memory clearly displayed on his face.

"A few weeks later, I arrived at work early and was reading the online headlines. An image of Teddy popped up. It took me a minute to remember where I knew him from." He inhales raggedly. "Teddy was struck by a bullet and killed." His voice catches on his last word. There are audible gasps from the audience.

"Teddy was with his stepbrother. The two were walking home with groceries for their mom, and a fourteen-year-old kid shot at them. His stepbrother was hit in the arm. Teddy was struck in the head." Luke takes a drink of the water Maggie hands him. "His death hit me harder than I would have ever thought possible. I thought about him a lot over the next few days. It dawned on me that if that kid-turned-murderer had been involved with Second Chances, Teddy might still be alive. I returned that very next Saturday, but this time I was doing it for the right reasons. I understood in my heart that these kids needed to be there, and maybe I did too."

Several people wipe tears from the corners of their eyes.

"I want to close by thanking you for this opportunity, and I want to encourage everyone here tonight to do their part to prevent anymore premature deaths of children in our community. Help with your time if you can. Help with your bank account if you can. We all have something to offer, and we owe it to our community and these kids to help."

Luke receives a standing ovation for his moving speech. He returns to our table as Maggie gives instructions on ways to donate.

Luke puts his hand on my shoulder and smiles at me when I peer up at him. He sits and takes a drink of his wine before leaning back in his chair. I don't sense any arrogance from him, only gratitude.

After donation forms have been filled out, conversation at our table resumes. Andi recounts a lively story about a new client who has hired her to develop a full marketing plan for their craft beer business. The owner keeps insisting the slogan should be "We Give the Best Head in Town," despite her repeated efforts to convince him otherwise.

Our entire table is laughing when the band starts playing. Couples abandon their table conversations and cups of coffee to hit the dance floor. Aaron is the first at our table to stand and take Andi's hand.

"Let's get some air." Luke rises and extends a hand out to me.

I take it and follow him to the three sets of glass doors that lead out onto the massive ballroom balcony. It seems no one else has found this spot yet. The damp autumn air is refreshing as we exit into the night.

"I liked your speech." We stop near the railing. Luke turns around and leans his back against it.

"Thanks." He shrugs.

"You didn't mention what we were coming here for tonight. I should have asked. You're doing something admirable with this group. You should be proud."

"I'm proud of the work that Second Chances does. I merely help out where I can. I don't like to go around talking about it. I guess I've always thought that would cheapen it somehow or sound like I'm patting myself on the back. That speech tonight is the first time I've shared the story of how I got involved."

"I'm glad I was here for it."

"Me too."

A loud group of men bursts through the glass doors. It appears the secret is out about this spot, so we return to the party. A table of young women whisper and giggle as we walk by their table. Luke seems to draw as much attention in San Francisco as he does in Temecula.

"I need to find the restroom," I say to Luke as we approach the bar.

"I'll get you a glass of red wine and meet you back at the table."

"That would be great, thanks."

In the reception area, I see a sign indicating the women's restroom is around the corner. I'm having a better time tonight than I thought I would. I may even be glad I came.

I'm relieved to find no line. I have just entered one of the empty stalls when my ears are assaulted by the shrieking and giggling of women who have decided to bring their party into the restroom. I continue with my business and pay no attention to their boisterous conversation. I'm finishing up when I hear Luke's name in their exchange.

"Oh my God, Jackie! You can't say that!" one of them shouts.

"What? It's true!" Another is laughing so hard, she barely gets the words out.

"Please tell me he did not do that! Please tell me you did not let him do that to you!"

"Have you seen him? Don't even pretend that you wouldn't have let him too!"

"No way. He's hot, but I'm not doing that with anyone."

Another one of the hens joins the conversation. "That's probably why you only had one night with him, Becky. He had to move on to someone more adventurous."

"Listen, we all know Luke Taylor isn't boyfriend material. One fun night is what most of us get with him."

"Well, I've had more than one, and they've all been hot as hell. Maybe you just couldn't keep up."

I pray for a fire alarm to go off so they're forced to evacuate and possibly even get hosed down during the process. Unfortunately, I'm forced to listen to details so crude, I must remind myself they aren't talking about a porn movie they saw. Apparently they have all had a turn with the town's most eligible bachelor. They compare notes on foreplay, positions, length of activity, and props used. I pinch my arm to test if I'm lucky enough to wake up from this nightmare. I'm not.

It feels like time moves in slow motion, until they finally leave. I'm not sure what's going to be the worst part of this evening, having to listen to multiple sex stories about Luke, or facing him with my new, unwanted knowledge.

Chapter 10

I've been in here too long. I reluctantly decide it's time to go back to the ballroom, even if for no other reason than to retrieve my purse from the table. My mother always told me to never leave my purse unattended. If I had listened to her advice, I would have it with me right now and would be able to escape without having to deal with Luke.

A showdown with him is not a good idea. I want no part of being a grown woman causing a scene at a respectable fundraising gala. The mature way to handle this is to bite my tongue and get the hell out of here.

I'm not surprised when I find Luke waiting for me when I exit the restroom.

"Everything okay? I was beginning to worry about you."

"Yep." I answer simply, afraid if I speak too many words my anger will show through them.

"Good. I'm really glad you're here tonight." He gives me a full smile.

He's confident he has me right where he wants me. My pride overrides my desire to avoid confrontation. I have an intense desire to knock him down a few notches.

"You are disgusting, and I am leaving," I announce matter-of-factly.

Luke lets out an incredulous laugh. "Okay…clearly I missed something." He raises his hands in front of him as I storm past him. "Hey, wait." He follows me back to our table. I picture a puzzled expression on his face, but I don't know for sure because I don't look back. At the table, I quickly grab my purse and spin around.

Luke's eyes widen when I glare at him. "Talk to me. What's going on?" He reaches out to touch my arm, but I pull back out of reach.

"Do not touch me." I'm careful not to raise my voice above the clatter of the room. "This was a mistake. I wish you well. What you're doing here with the charity is amazing, but I have to go." I walk past him toward the elevators.

"Will you please wait a minute?" He follows me again through the ballroom. "We were having a nice evening, and then all of a sudden, you're acting like you found out I murdered someone."

We walk past a table of young women. They're all batting their fake eyelashes at him. They're obviously the ladies from the restroom. My stomach churns.

I will give Luke credit for not being a complete idiot. He quickly assesses the situation. "Shit…wait." He continues to chase me to the elevator. "At least have a conversation with me."

I don't respond until I have pressed the down button. "I will not discuss this here. Not in front of these good people and definitely not in front of your…fan club." I wave an arm at the ballroom, where Luke's harem has undoubtedly returned to their glasses of chardonnay and boring dates.

He follows me in as I step into the elevator but doesn't dare say anything. The door closes, and we stand in uncomfortable silence. I consider telling him to go back to the party, but Luke is not easily deterred, and he clearly intends on talking about this sooner than later. I need to deal with him directly, but the conversation will wait until we have some privacy.

I try to appreciate the quiet as we walk to his car, knowing what comes next isn't going to be pleasant. When the driver emerges to open the rear door for us, Luke waves him off. He opens it himself, and I slide in past him. Once he's settled inside too, he instructs the driver to drive us back to his apartment. The driver nods and closes the partition.

"All right, let's talk." He rubs the back of his neck.

"No thanks." I turn and gaze out the window at the passing city. It's easier to stand my ground when I'm not looking at him. Besides, I could use a few more minutes to steady my emotions.

"No thanks?" He sounds bewildered. "That's not an acceptable response."

"You, sir, are in no position to lecture me about acceptable behavior." A fake cackle escapes from my throat.

Luke sighs. "I knew this would come up sooner or later. Obviously, I was hoping for later, but…"

I forget my strategy in an instant and turn my scowl at him. "Oh, I'm sure you were. My guess is the fact that you've slept with the entire city wasn't something you were planning on sharing with me."

"I haven't slept with the entire city and I knew I was going to have to share my past with you at some point, just maybe not this weekend." Luke shakes his head. "I've been a single man for a long time—"

"I don't know where you're going with this, but excuse me for thinking that sticking your dick in anyone who will let you is repulsive." My voice is louder than I intend. "You're lucky it hasn't fallen off."

"First and foremost, I always protect myself—"

"Stop. I really don't want to hear anymore right now." My face must convey the emotions that are threatening to explode from me, because Luke sighs and closes his mouth. "Why am I even here? You clearly have enough activity to keep yourself busy for a very long time. I don't understand what kind of woman you think I am, but I'll tell you who I'm not. I'm not a woman who shares sex stories in a bathroom and laughs about sharing a man with all my girlfriends."

"You know that's not what I think." Luke frowns.

"Do I? It's become very apparent I know very little about you, what you think, and how you live your life. I would never sleep with half the men in the room and then try to convince you you're special and different."

"My sleeping with other women doesn't invalidate my feelings for you. I would've rather been with you than any of them." Luke purses his lips together when he looks at me. "I would've been with you, but you went and fell in love with someone else."

"Don't you dare! You left. What was I supposed to do?" He flinches, and I turn away.

Seconds turn into minutes as we sit in stillness and struggle with what comes next. I can't come up with anything else to say. I realize I'm furiously twirling my hair around a finger and force myself to stop.

"I'm sorry." His words hang in the air. I remain silent and focus on the cars driving next to us for a few more minutes.

Once I've calmed down I respond. "It's not my place to say anything about your lifestyle. I just think you're better than that. You have much more to offer than that."

"Of course I do. I haven't wanted to offer anything more."

We don't talk for the remainder of the drive to Luke's apartment. I suspect it's not because neither of us has anything to say, but because there is too much to say. Too much that still needs to be said, things our exhausted hearts and heads are not prepared to hear tonight.

"Thank you, Dean," Luke says after we exit the car. He waves to his driver, and we enter his building.

In the elevator, Luke lets out a frustrated sigh. "Well, tonight didn't play out how I envisioned in my head."

"I imagine not."

"I really thought that if we spent some time together…" Luke leans against the elevator wall.

"Luke—"

He raises a hand to stop my thought. "It's been a long night. I have to be honest. I'm out of my element here. I've never had this much trouble with, well, anyone."

"I'm sorry."

"Why are you apologizing? There's nothing you need to be sorry about."

"This should've been a night to celebrate you being appointed to the board."

"I don't care about the recognition. I only care about one person's opinion of me at the moment."

"I don't want to mislead you. I don't know if there is anything left for us." I'm so confused. I try to be as honest as I can. "I need to be cautious."

"I understand. I've been cautious too, just in a different way."

I sigh and look down at my shoes. "Luke, I'm not sure we're meant to have some storybook ending. I stopped believing in fairy tales a long time ago. Real life doesn't play out that way."

"Fairy tales may not be real, but I do believe some people wind up with a happy ending."

We exit the elevator and enter his apartment.

"Good night, Luke."

"Good night."

For the first time, I hear a whisper of defeat in his voice.

Despite my tiredness, I can't sleep. I make a pros and cons list regarding giving Luke and me another chance. When that doesn't work, I try to not think about him at all. I download and begin to read a new novel. After twenty minutes, I realize I remember nothing about the last ten pages I just read and turn off my phone. I thought relationship stuff was supposed to be easier to handle as an adult. I feel like I'm fourteen years old again...indecisive and downright frightened of my emotions.

Maybe a warm drink will help. It's late. I'm sure Luke has already gone to bed. I get up, determined to find my way back to the kitchen.

I'm surprised when I open the bedroom door to see the glow from the fireplace. Luke is sitting on the couch. My entrance startles him, and his head jerks up from the paper he is reading.

"I didn't think you'd still be up. I didn't...I didn't mean to bother you." I'm already confused about my feelings for him, and his half-naked body isn't helping. He's wearing pajama pants but no shirt. The light from the fire dances across his bare chest, illuminating exactly how muscular he is.

"No problem. I was catching up on some work." He sets his laptop aside and stands.

When he does, I see the definition of his Adonis belt. He did not have that in high school. He is not overly big, but he clearly works out. By the time my eyes reach his face, he is smirking. I'm mortified I was so blatant in my admiration of his body.

"Do you want something, Jessica?" I hear a subtle hint of seduction in his voice, and heat rises in me. I don't know if he means to do it or if it's my imagination that assumes everything he says is laced with sexual innuendo. I shake my own dirty thoughts and remember what I came out here for.

"I'm in search of tea. You know, to drink? Like chamomile or something? I'm having trouble falling asleep and thought it may help. Sometimes when I can't sleep, a cup of hot tea does the trick." I'm rambling and should stop, but the words keep spilling out.

"Sure." He takes off to the kitchen.

I follow him and take a seat at the counter bar. He searches through one of the cupboards and grabs a box of tea bags from a top shelf. The motions make his back muscles move and flex. Up until this moment, I never thought a man's back could be called sexy. My eyes are drawn to the waistband of his pajama pants. I wonder what he looks like under them. It's been a very long time since I've seen Luke naked. Not to mention that his body has changed in some very exciting ways.

Without warning, Luke shoots me a glance over his shoulder. He smiles knowingly. "Quit checking me out." He takes the honey out of the cabinet as well.

What's wrong with me? I need to get ahold of myself and stop ogling him, even if he likes it. His familiar words make my heart ache though. Did he use those same exact words from the day we met on purpose, or was it merely a coincidence?

Before I have a chance to open my mouth and undoubtedly embarrass myself further, he says, "Chamomile tea with one spoonful of honey and a splash of milk?"

"Yeah. How did you know that?"

"I remember a lot of things about you."

I don't know if it's the heat from the fireplace, being so close to him and his half-naked body, or that he can be so charming, but it is suddenly very warm inside the apartment.

He finishes making my tea and hands me the cup. He leans back against the kitchen counter as I sip the sweet, creamy liquid.

He clears his throat. "About those women tonight...I'm really sorry you had to hear that. I've lived my life unapologetically the last ten years because I didn't believe my actions were hurting anyone. I certainly didn't know my behavior was ever going to cause you any pain. If I would've thought I would ever be having this conversation with you..." He trails off.

"It wasn't fun to hear, but it really isn't any of my business. I'm not in a position to have an opinion on how you've lived your life."

"Of course you're going to have an opinion about it. I hope you can see beyond that though. I wanted us to have a nice weekend. A chance to remember the good and not only the bad, but I guess we'll have to relive some of both."

I take a deep breath before bringing up the topic that causes him the most pain. "Luke, I can't be sorry about my marriage and my life with Grant."

He shakes his head and crosses his strong arms across his chest. "Of course not. I shouldn't have said anything about that. You don't owe me any kind of explanation."

"I didn't even know about your feelings after we broke up and I started dating him."

"No, because I never told you. That was my fault."

"Yes, but knowing how you felt does explain some things. I can't wish things had turned out differently, but maybe now we can both get some closure."

"I'm not looking for closure." He gazes straight at me, arms still crossed.

"I know you're not."

"But you are?"

"I don't know. Maybe that's all that we can get out of this."

He shakes his head. "I don't think so. And deep down, you don't think that either."

"How do you know that?" I tilt my head.

He pushes away from the counter and leans across the bar. "Because you're here. That you even came here means you have some inkling this is a beginning and not an ending."

"Maybe this is all too complicated, too painful for both of us." I take another sip of tea, and my gaze drops to the marble countertop.

"Life is complicated. If great things were easy, everyone would do them."

I lift my eyes back up to meet his. "Luke, I can't promise you anything right now."

"I'm not asking you to. I'm not doing a great job of reassuring you this is right, but I am going to."

I don't respond to his bold assertion. I have always admired his ability to be absolutely certain about things. I don't have that. Unfortunately, his unwavering belief in us is non-transferable. Sometimes wanting something to be true isn't enough to make it so.

I finish my tea and return to the guest bedroom. This time I fall right to sleep and dream about Luke in his pajama pants.

Chapter 11

I awake to sounds of light knocking on the bedroom door. It takes me a minute to interpret my surroundings. Dull light peeks through the blinds, indicating it is morning. It's either really early or cloudy outside.

I could tell him to go away, but I've never knowingly fought a losing battle. I make sure I'm still fully covered by the fluffy blanket I spent the night wrapped up in.

"Come in," I say warily as I reclose my eyes.

His head appears first. I open one eye. If he's going to wake me up, he better have caffeine. He pushes the door fully open. He has a bag in one hand and a mug in the other. He sets the coffee on the nightstand. I can't resist its seductive smell and rise to a sitting position. I take a small sip to make sure it's not too hot. I usually prefer tea, but this is perhaps the best cup of coffee I've ever had. I take another taste and enjoy the heated liquid running down my throat. I imagine it warming my entire soul as it wakes me up and soothes me at the same time. I release a small throaty "mmm."

"I've never seen anyone drink coffee like that." He is staring at my mouth.

My goal was not to draw any attention to myself, so his comment makes me blush.

He clears his throat. "My assistant picked these up for you. Get dressed and we'll go for a run." He sets the bag on the end of the bed. I only now notice he has running clothes on.

"I don't run anymore." I take another mouthful of heaven in liquid form.

"I was afraid of that." Luke frowns. "Well, today you start again. Meet you downstairs in thirty minutes." He leaves and shuts the door.

I'm not shocked he wants to go for a run. It was something I grew to enjoy in high school, but I stopped many years ago. This is going to be painful, definitely physically and probably emotionally. I'm curious about what topics may come up during our run though, so I will join him…after I finish my coffee.

I join Luke out front, where he is stretching. I bend and pull my limbs in an attempt to coax them to loosen up. After several minutes, I'm warming up despite the chilliness of the damp morning air.

The first ten minutes are awful, and I consider quitting with each stride. I can't decide which is burning more, my lungs or my legs. I can't remember why I ever enjoyed this. I make deals with myself along the way, like if I make it to that next tree, I'll stop. If I make it past the next building, I'll tell Luke I'm turning around. But I don't stop. I just keep making new deals.

Eventually the endorphins kick in, and everything seems less painful. My thoughts drift to the subject that haunts me daily—my impending divorce. Ever since I found those texts on Grant's phone, I have been carrying around a heaviness. I know others have felt it and even attempted to talk to me about it, but I haven't been ready to let go of it. In a weird way, the sadness makes me feel safer. It's a reminder not to put myself in a position where I could experience this level of pain again. This is the first time I've admitted this to myself. I cringe because it doesn't sound healthy even in my own head.

My body tells me it's time to stop when I get a sharp pain in my side. I slow, and Luke stops running too. We walk up the block and land in front of a small bakery. I inhale the scents of butter and sugar as I walk in a circle and continue to cool down. Luke paces back and forth but isn't nearly as fatigued as I am.

He examines the pedometer on his wrist. "Three miles. Not bad, Adams."

I remember a time when I heard similar words.

I've told Luke a thousand times I'm not a runner. I learned to avoid PE class after Ricky Garcia threw a ball at me during a third grade game of dodge ball that pegged me right in the face. The other kids laughed, and I thought I was going to die from humiliation. Since then, I participated as little as possible in any game involving balls flying near my head. Even though I was unlikely to be hit in the head while running, my loathing of physical education expanded to include it as well.

"Just one run? I promise, if you really hate it, I won't bug you to do it again." Luke smiled at me like he already knew I was going to give in to his request. He always got his way.

"Fine. One run. But I'm not a runner, so I'm not going to be able to keep up with you." I already regretted my decision.

"I'll run behind you. You can set the pace, and I'll enjoy the view," he said with a naughty grin.

"Oh no, you won't!" I shrieked at him, and he laughed. "You run ahead of me. I'm just warning you that I'll need to stop before you will."

"Okay. I run in front, and we stop when you need to. Any other demands?"

"I don't think so. When are we going on this dreaded jog?" I continued taking notes from the United States history text-book in front of me.

"Let's go now." Luke popped up from where he'd been lying on my bedroom floor.

"I can't go now," I protested, but I could already see the familiar look of determination on his face. He was unstoppable once he set his mind on something.

He fetched my shoes from the closet, ignoring my attempt to delay the inevitable.

I reluctantly went to the bathroom to change, and when I emerged, he was gone. I looked out my window and saw him waiting outside. I begrudgingly headed downstairs and let my mom know we were going for a run. She started to say something but stopped when she saw I was wearing one of the few things I own that qualified as a workout outfit. She gave me a puzzled look. I shrugged my shoulders and headed out the front door.

As promised, he maintained a pace that surely felt tur-tle-slow to him but allowed me to keep up. I stopped a couple of times, and so did he. Eventually I found a rhythm of sorts and pushed myself a little harder. I finally stopped when my lungs felt like they might burst into flames.

"That was almost two miles. Not bad for your first time, Adams." He examined his pedometer while I caught my breath.

"So, what do you really want to do with your life?" His question seemed to come out of nowhere and caught me off guard.

"What?"

"Like, what would truly make you happy?"

"I'm going to study business in college," I answered. "You already know that."

"That's not what I asked. What would make you happy?"

"Like, if earning a viable living wasn't a goal?"

"Exactly."

"I don't know." He appeared truly interested, so I put a little more thought into my answer. "I enjoy taking pictures. I've sometimes daydreamed about being a successful photographer."

"That's cool. You've never mentioned this before."

"Well, I also want to be able to afford more than ramen for dinner every night, so business is a safer option." The question still felt random to me. "Why are you asking me this now?"

"I have this theory about running, that when your legs are aching and your lungs are burning, you can't think of much else. It clears your mind of all the clutter. I like to run before I make any big decision. Then I know I'm making a decision based on my true feelings and not letting other junk get in the way." He shrugged and looked down at his feet.

A realization dawned on me. "This is why you wanted me to go running with you? Why didn't you tell me?"

"I thought it would sound, well, dumb. I thought if you experienced it, you would know what I was feeling, and it would make more sense."

Luke and I started going on weekly runs together. We discussed our dreams and fears. We learned a lot about ourselves and each other. I continued to run, even after he left, until I found out I was pregnant. Once I married Grant and had Amelia, I never made time for it again.

"Jessica?" Luke says my name in a way that leads me to believe this isn't the first time he's said it.

"What?"

"I asked you if it helped?" He's eyeing me cautiously.

Tears pool in my eyes, but I'm able to wipe them away before they overflow.

"What is it?" He sounds genuinely concerned.

"I don't know."

"Just say what you need to say."

"Why did you take me on this run?"

Luke sighs and takes a few steps toward me. "I'm trying to help. You're holding back, and it's hurting you more than it's helping."

"I'm scared." The truth spills out before I think better of it.

"Of what exactly?"

"A lot of things. Things I'm not ready to share with you." I shake my head and focus on controlling my tears.

"Fair enough. I probably haven't earned the right to ask that. Maybe you're not ready to tell me what you're feeling, but you need to at least be honest with yourself."

Luke is quiet for several minutes. He's always been good about knowing when to push and when to back off. I suspect that's one reason why he's a successful negotiator.

"My turn to ask you some questions." I change the subject.

"What's on your mind?" he asks without a trace of hesitation.

"We've run into each other a lot over the last few months. How have you been able to show up where I'm at?"

"Can you be more specific?" His mischievous grin gives him away before his words do.

"Well, you showed up at my work after the reunion, and you admitted that wasn't a coincidence."

"That's not a question," he teases. He appears to be enjoying where this conversation is heading.

"How did you know I was going to be at the bar with my friends that night?"

"That time actually was coincidental. Like I told you that night, my assistant came to attend meetings with me. We were grabbing a quick drink at the end of a long day. You being there was a pleasant surprise."

"Pleasant isn't how I would describe it. Apparently, I don't remember the evening the same way you do."

"Obviously not. I remember I got to drive you home."

"She's very pretty, your assistant." I try extra hard to make it sound like a simple observation and not the words of a jealous woman.

"I know where you're going with this, and no, I haven't slept with her. Contrary to what you're thinking, I've never mixed my dating and professional lives."

"Isn't that exactly what we're doing?"

"That's not fair. You're different. I will break every one of my rules for you."

My chest involuntarily tightens. "All right. Amelia's soccer game? That couldn't have been a coincidence."

"It wasn't. It's not that difficult to find out where local youth soccer games are being held. I went to a different field first. I got lucky that the second field was the right one." Luke wears a cocky grin and appears to be very proud of himself.

"Some people might consider this stalking." I raise my eyebrows.

"Only if you're creepy. In my case, I consider it using my resources wisely."

"What about the Mexican food from my favorite restaurant?"

"That was a mix of detective work and luck. I had Aaron call Linda to see if she could recommend a great Mexican restaurant in town. I took a chance that you would like the same place. Glad to hear it's your favorite."

"Stalker." I can't help but smile at the idea of him going to so much trouble. The time feels right to admit something. "You know what I'm really afraid of?"

"What?"

"Making another mistake."

"What mistakes have you made?"

"I don't know. Maybe trusting people I shouldn't?"

"If you're talking about Grant, it's not your fault the guy you married turned out to be a cheating asshole. As much as I don't like the guy, I know better than to assume he's always been a dick. You married him because there was something real there. Just because it didn't work out doesn't mean you had bad judgment."

"I don't know if you're the best one to be judging people about monogamy."

"Wait a minute. Let's be clear. I'm not like him. I purposely have chosen not to be in relationships, specifically so no one gets hurt. When I commit, I don't cheat."

"I wish I could be more casual like that."

"No, you don't." Luke shakes his head.

"Seems like it's been working for you."

"Has it? Is that why I'm working so hard to convince you to give me another chance?" He raises an eyebrow.

"So why are you? We've both had the opportunity to say things we needed to say and clear the air. We could be friends."

"No offense but I have enough friends. I know there's something still here. Something worth exploring."

"How can you be so sure?"

"I just am."

"I wish I was too. I may be too damaged to even think about getting into another relationship." I lower my gaze, ashamed of the words that just came out of my mouth.

Luke closes the space between us. At first I think he's going to kiss me. Instead he stands in front of me and places his hands on my shoulders. "You're not damaged Jessica, you're hurt and scared." He looks at me intently, making sure I'm paying attention. "If a time comes when you tell me you don't want to be with me, I will leave you alone. You're going to be fine with or without me, but I hope I'm still here when you remember how amazing you are and are ready for something more."

He wraps both arms around me. His arms are strong, and his body is warm. There is nothing sexual about this hug; it's simply comforting. When I move, he releases me. The look on his face says he's concerned we're saying goodbye. I'm not ready to tell him I'm afraid to let him leave.

Chapter 12

On our walk back to Luke's apartment, I alternate between going home and staying. Both options cause my anxiety to swell. I'm attracted to him and afraid of him. My fear of being hurt again feels paralyzing. I decide to stay, partially because it requires the least amount of effort.

Luke tells me he's made plans for us this evening, but he's keeping it a surprise. My attempts to convince him to tell me where we're going only succeeds in adding to his enjoyment of the situation.

"At least tell me what I should wear," I say, mock frustrated.

"I vote for nothing." I punch him in his arm, and he laughs. "Jeans and heels." He pretends to tend to his injured arm. I'm guessing any shoes would be fine, but he's always had a thing for heels.

He smiles at the building security guard as we approach. "Good morning, Mr. Taylor."

"Good morning, Gus. You agreed to start calling me Luke."

"Sure thing, Mr. Taylor."

Luke laughs, and we step into the elevator. "Unfortunately, I have work I have to finish today. I tried to get it done last night, but there are a few more items that can't wait until Monday." Luke pushes the button that will send us up to his apartment.

"Not a problem." I could use some quiet time.

"I planned on us having an uninterrupted weekend, but one of our companies experienced unexpected personnel changes, and everyone went into crisis management mode."

"I understand, and it's fine."

"I can have Dean drive you wherever you'd like to go," Luke offers. He feels guilty, but he doesn't need to.

"I appreciate the offer, but I think I'll just relax."

He retreats to his office, and I take a long, steaming bath and read several chapters of a book on my phone. I add hot water more than once. My fingers and toes are shriveled by the time I drag myself out. I select a pair of fitted jeans, a low-cut black silk top, and a pair of black strappy heels. I have to admit his assistant has great taste. I still have time to spare, so I curl my hair. I'm halfway through when I remember Luke used to like my hair curled. I retrieve a small black purse from the closet and put my cell phone, ID, credit card, and lipstick inside.

When I enter the living room, I don't see him right away. I spot him standing by the large windows in the dining room. He appears deep in thought and hasn't noticed me yet. If I take another step, he will hear me and turn around, so I freeze. I want a minute to enjoy him. He is refined but casual. His jeans and dark blue sweater fit perfectly, like all his clothes.

He catches my reflection in the window and turns around. "Adams," he breathes out at the sight of me. I've come to accept his use of my maiden name as a term of endearment.

"I'm ready to go," I blurt.

"Okay." He winks.

I catch him watching me several times on our way downstairs. He must have already given the driver instructions, because he doesn't say anything to him when we get in the car. I'm disappointed. I was hoping to get a clue to our destination.

Once we're on our way, Luke starts talking. "My plan is to not compliment you too much tonight. It seems to make you uncomfortable, and I want you to have fun." Luke smiles at me and widens his eyes. "Although you're definitely not making this any easier for me when you show up looking like that."

"Thank you." I decided during my bath that my goal this evening is to try to be as relaxed as possible. It's my hope that an evening without emotional drama will give me perspective.

"You're welcome." Luke taps his foot.

"Still not going to tell me where we're going?"

"Nope. Foreplay is half the fun."

"You're terrible. I thought you wanted me to relax." I frown at him in an over-exaggerated way. Our playfulness is helping me feel more at ease.

"Sorry, I'll try harder." He tries to suppress it, but the corners of his mouth curl up slightly.

He asks questions about Amelia and my work, two topics I'm most confident discussing. I'm sure they weren't chosen by accident. His strategy works, and I'm more comfortable with him already. I'm telling him about the time Amelia tried to save a stray dog by bringing him into our house when his phone rings.

"Don't stop." He turns off his phone.

"You can get that. I don't mind."

"It was Aaron. I can talk to him tomorrow. Tonight I want to focus on...oh wait, that's right. You don't know where we're going," he teases.

We've only been driving for twenty minutes or so when the driver exits the freeway. I eagerly try to determine where we are.

We pull into the parking lot of Oracle Arena, so I assume we're going to a basketball game. It's an unexpected date choice since I don't follow the game, but it should still be a fun evening. As soon as I see the marquee, I understand why he's been keeping tonight under wraps.

"I saw they were playing, and I know you like them." Luke attempts to sound nonchalant about bringing me here tonight.

I nervously pick at my nails.

"If this is too much, we can simply go to dinner or go do something else."

He knows this is too much, but he also knows I'm not going to say no to a Maroon 5 concert. He's not playing fair.

"This is great. I do love them. Thank you." I give him a wide smile and place a hand on my knee to stop it from bouncing. Even though I worry what this night will do to me, I can't help but be excited.

The driver drops us off, and we find our seats. I'm not surprised they're on the floor. We still have thirty minutes before the show begins, so we hit the bar. We order gin and tonics. I down my first one. Its burn is welcome and distracts me from my feelings.

We return to our seats as the lights go down, and the opening act takes the stage. They are a local band I'm not familiar with, but they're good, and I enjoy their set.

During intermission, we return to the bar for more drinks. We pass people our age wearing concert T-shirts from back when we were in high school, complete with jeans that obviously date back to that era. We laugh, reminiscing about what we wore back then. The night is going better than I expected, and I'm more at ease than I had hoped. I'm glad I didn't go home today, and I'm happy Luke planned this date.

We return to our seats once again as the lights are dimming. Maroon 5 takes the stage. They play, and I dance and sing along to every song. During their older songs, I feel like I've been transported back to my teen years. I experience the excitement, the rush, the confusion, the angst…all of it. It's overwhelming, but I breathe through it, taking it all in. I let go and allow myself to get immersed in the music. It makes me feel alive, like myself again. I haven't felt like this in a long time.

They haven't played it yet, but I know what song is coming up. I know what it will bring to the surface. I don't want this night to be ruined because of another emotional display by me, so I decide it's a good time to excuse myself to the restroom.

I'm finishing up when the familiar notes fill the air. It's our song. "She Will be Loved" was playing when we danced and he whispered for the first time that he loved me. Even in a room full of students and teachers, it was the most intimate, romantic moment of my fifteen-year-old life. I still can't hear the song without remembering that night. I listen to the words. As a teenager, I focused on the chorus. I took the words at face value and interpreted them as an expression of Luke's love for me. Presently, the plea to not try so hard to say goodbye stands out more. When the song ends, I compose myself and make my way back to him.

As I approach the door leading back into the concert, I see Luke. He's leaning against the opposite wall, eyes cast down. He raises his eyes to mine when I'm standing in front of him. "Everything okay?"

"Yeah. They're really amazing live." I keep my voice light. Maybe some appreciation will stop him from looking at me with such sadness. "I'm having a great time. Thank you again for planning this."

"That's not what I meant. Never mind." He pushes away from the wall and walks away.

"Wait," I call after him. He pauses and turns around, but I don't know what to say next, so we only look at each other. He shakes his head and turns away. "Wait," I say again. "What's wrong?" It's a stupid question, because I know what's wrong.

"Nothing. Let's go back in." He doesn't look back at me as he continues toward the door.

"Will you please wait?" I yell this time, and he stops.

"Why?" he snaps. He turns around while rubbing his face. "Sorry, this is not the plan."

"What is the plan?"

"Certainly not this." He throws his hands up in an "I give up" gesture. "Things are never this hard for me…ever. I don't know what to do, okay? I don't know how to fix…" He waves back and forth between us. "And that fucking song. Does that song hold any meaning for you anymore? Does it make you feel anything?" He squints his eyes at me.

"Of course it does. You're clearly upset with me. If there's something you need to say, go ahead and say it." I brace myself.

"I don't have a problem saying it, but you have a problem hearing it."

"I'm ready." I'm not, but I'm ready to rip this bandage off.

"When did you last hear that song?" He wraps his arms across his chest.

"I don't know," I lie. It came on the radio a month ago, while I was driving Amelia to school one morning. I covered and said my allergies must be acting up when my eyes began to water.

"No? Well, I do. I remember the exact moment I last heard that song. You know why? Because I have never listened to it in its entirety since." Luke lets out a rush of air. "I heard it at that damn party. The night I saw you with Grant. It was on when I walked into the house. I thought it was a sign we were supposed to be there that night." He appears to be deciding whether to continue or not. "I was so angry when I saw you with him, I almost told him to get his hands off my girl…but I didn't." He closes his eyes. "I left and sulked and decided that song was cursed. I knew we'd hear it tonight. I knew it would stir up feelings in me. I thought maybe it would stir up feelings in you too."

"Luke…" I reach out to touch him, but he takes a step back.

"Listen, I've been in love with you since I was fifteen years old. Yes, I fucked it up, and I know that. I see the possibility of something great between us, something life changing, but you don't. Or you don't want to."

I start to respond, but he cuts me off.

"I don't want to wait anymore. I've already spent too much of my life without you in it. I thought I could show you this weekend. I thought I could get you to remember how good we are together. I don't want to let you go again. Please tell me I don't have to." His eyes are wet, and he's wearing the most heartbreaking expression I've ever seen.

The look on his face makes me decide in an instant. Any doubts I ever had about his intentions seem absurd at this point. I grab him by his sweater and kiss him hard. His body reacts before his brain does, and he kisses me back with equal fervor, wrapping his arms tightly around me.

He releases my mouth but maintains his hold on me. "I can't do casual with you, not with you."

"Did that feel casual? We both know there are too many feelings involved for that."

He kisses me again but breaks contact too early. I need more. "We need to get out of here." He leads me outside and texts his driver. He pulls me into his chest as we wait on the sidewalk. "I want to be alone with you, but we can take this as slow as you want to."

"I think being apart for ten years is slow enough." I stand on my tiptoes and whisper in his ear. "I want you now."

I hear Luke's sharp inhalation right as the car pulls up.

We get in, and he raises the privacy partition.

"Are you sure?" He is breathing hard.

"Yes. Absolutely yes." My own breathing is difficult to regulate.

"One more question." He rakes his eyes over my body. The anticipation makes me tingle. "Now, or wait until we get back to the apartment? Honest answer please, because it's going to be difficult to stop once we start."

My body is tingling and I only need a second to consider my answer. "Now."

I lean back, and he climbs on top of me. He kisses me fully and deeply. I don't remember ever being kissed quite like this. I remind myself to keep breathing.

"I apologize in advance for being too eager during round one." He unbuttons my blouse, watching me closely. He's tentative, like he's afraid I'm going to change my mind. I give him no indication of doing so, and he moves his mouth down to my collarbone.

"Round one?" I manage to mumble.

"Uh-huh." He hums against my already sensitized skin.

"That's what they all say." I'm already overwhelmed, so I attempt to insert some humor.

He lifts his head. "They do, do they? Well, it sounds like 'they' have never followed through on their promises. I always do." He winks and undoes my jeans.

It's evident he's trying to pace himself and not just rip my clothes off. He pauses between buttons, zippers, and clasps to place kisses on whatever body part he has bared. He removes my jeans and then my blouse. After he takes my bra off, he puts his mouth on my already hardened nipple and sucks. Electricity courses through me, and I can't help but moan. I feel his mouth smile against my skin before drawing my nipple back inside. I wonder if it's possible to orgasm from this alone.

He doesn't break suction as he reaches down to remove my panties. Only once he's stretched his arms as far as they will go does he remove his mouth from my breast. He finishes with the panties and gazes at my completely naked body.

"Fucking gorgeous." Luke lowers his head between my legs. He lifts my legs up at the knees and spreads them apart, giving him full access.

He begins with a light lick. After a few more, he changes his approach to include kisses. He lets a kiss linger and gently pulls me into his mouth. He quickly releases me and repeats the sequence again. My pleasure is building, and I can't control the noises I make to let him know it.

He continues his assault until my breath is ragged and my hips are thrusting toward him. He reaches up with one hand and squeezes my nipple. The sensation distracts me for a moment, so I'm surprised when he slides his fingers inside me. I arch and rasp out something unintelligible.

"You taste so good. I want you to come in my mouth." He lowers his head again. This time he's more aggressive. He thrusts his fingers faster and sucks harder. The combination of sensations makes me climax suddenly and forcefully. He continues to suck as I ride out the waves rippling through me. As I'm winding down, he releases me and takes off his jeans. I feel a little guilty for not helping, but I feel weak and shaky. He finishes removing his boxer briefs and catches me admiring the view. He grins at me in a way that makes my insides fire up again.

"I needed to be inside you, like, thirty minutes ago. I promise I'll take better care of you once we're back at the apartment." He pulls a condom from the pocket of his jeans.

He moves me to the floor, and I give him a lazy smile and nod to let him know it's all right to proceed. After the condom is on, he enters me quickly and fully. Coming fresh off an orgasm, I'm quickly able to acclimate to his size. He moves with power and determination. I wrap my legs around him and use my muscles to grip him as he pounds into me.

His moans fuel my arousal. I continue to squeeze him as he thrusts. A few minutes later, he tenses and then releases. He collapses on me, and we stay like this for a moment, both relaxed after finally releasing our pent-up sexual energy.

His head is on my shoulder. "Do you think we would have to wait another ten years for it to ever be that amazing again?"

"Are you already trying to get out of your promises?" I tease. "We're only getting started."

Chapter 13

Luke follows through on his promise once we're back at his apartment. I don't know what I was expecting, but he's passionate and attentive. He looks at me with such adoration, I can't remember what I was so nervous about. By the end of the night we're exhausted, as much from our sexual activity as from the flood of emotions that has swept through our lives this weekend. I fall asleep easily while he strokes my hair.

I awaken to the smell of bacon. Drawn by the smells of breakfast and thoughts of Luke's amazing coffee, I'm motivated to remove myself from his cozy, disheveled bed. I search the room for something to throw on.

"Good morning," I announce as I enter the kitchen. He's at the stove, tending to scrambled eggs and bacon.

"Good"—he pauses when he sees me and smiles—"morning. My pajamas look good on you."

"Thanks." I sit at the counter.

"Hope you're hungry." He turns his attention back to the pans on the stove. Why is there something so sexy about a man cooking? It helps that he is also wearing a pair of his pajama bottoms and didn't bother to put a shirt on.

"Starving. Hey, do you happen to have any more of that—" Before I can finish my sentence, he places a mug of coffee in front of me. It already has milk in it and, I assume, the correct amount of sugar.

"I made you coffee. After watching you drink it last time, no way I was going to pass up an opportunity to see that again." He flips strips of bacon. "After breakfast we have a little time to clean up, but then we need to get to the airport."

"Okay." I never would have expected at the beginning of this weekend that I would be sad to see it come to an end. It has been a rollercoaster but worth it.

"Glad to see you smiling."

"I'm glad I came."

"I'm glad you came too...several times." He tries to hide it, but I catch a glimpse of his mischievous smile.

"You really are terrible," I say with a groan.

"But seriously, I was right about this weekend. We can both agree I have great instincts and should be the decision-maker of the relationship. In the future, we can avoid disagreements and save a lot of time if we agree I'm right and move on." His words drip with sarcasm.

"So you're saying I should simply agree with whatever you say going forward?" I pretend to consider his suggestion as I take another sip.

"It would save a lot of time and conserve our energy."

"Conserve our energy?"

"Yeah. We're going to have to find ways to conserve energy, so it can be used for more pleasurable pursuits." He plates the food and brings it to the counter.

"Let me see if I understand you correctly, you want me to agree with you so we don't waste time arguing, so we can have more sex?"

"That's ridiculous. I don't believe that's what I said at all." He sits across from me.

"Maybe I could quit my job and lie in bed all day, waiting for you to get home and have sex with me?" I sample the eggs. They're delicious.

Luke shrugs and picks up his fork. "That sounds very chauvinistic, but if that's what you want to do, I could support that."

I crumple my napkin and throw it at him. He catches it and sets it on the counter.

"When did you learn how to cook?" I ask, taking another bite of perfectly cooked bacon.

"I did pick up some new skills between the ages of nineteen and twenty-nine." Luke's comment is followed by an uncomfortable pause. "I didn't mean that to sound like it did."

I set my fork down and look at him. "We both have pasts. We're going to have to learn how to navigate this without constantly worrying about hurting the other person's feelings. Let's agree to take it easy on each other for now while we figure things out."

"Sounds good." Luke looks as relieved as I feel.

We finish our breakfast, discussing San Francisco and all the places he wants to show me when I come back. Despite his protests, I help clean up. I pour myself one more cup of coffee and make sure to take a picture of the bag in the cupboard so I can track it down later and order my own. My reconnection with Luke is the highlight of the weekend, but this coffee is a close second.

The rest of the morning is filled with mundane tasks like packing and showering. Well, showering would be mundane, but he decides to join me. I don't know why

I'm surprised. I suppose I figured he wouldn't be ready again so soon. After Grant and I had sex, he wouldn't be interested again for a while, sometimes weeks. Then again, we're getting divorced, so I probably shouldn't be using my experiences with Grant as any kind of bedroom activity barometer.

He holds my hand on the way to the airport and continues to hold it during most of the flight. We catch up on emails and texts, so we don't speak much, but the silence between us has already morphed into a comfortable one.

The pilot announces we're getting ready to descend. "When do I get to see you again?" he asks.

"I'm not sure." I haven't gotten that far in my planning today. I'm proud of myself for enjoying the moment and not overthinking too much.

"I have to fly to London tonight. I'm supposed to be gone until a week from Tuesday, but I can make arrangements to be back next weekend if you're free."

"I have Amelia next weekend." I hesitate. "I don't know if it's a good idea for you to meet her yet. Not as my…I mean as someone I'm…" I struggle to find the right words.

He squeezes my hand to halt my rambling. "First of all, I am yours. I meant it every time I said I don't want to be with anyone else, so please call me your boyfriend or whatever other title you want to give me." He smiles at me reassuringly and releases my hand. "Second, I get it. I'll officially meet her when you're ready."

"Thank you." My thoughts jump to another dilemma.

Luke senses my uneasiness. "What?"

"About work…"

"Now that's a different story. I have no intention of not telling everyone you're mine. I have waited a long time to be able to do that again, and I'm not wasting any time or energy on what others think. Neither should you."

"Calm down. It was only a thought. I just don't want to be the source of any gossip or to look bad in Mrs. Bianchi's eyes, that's all."

"People will always gossip. I plan on giving them lots to talk about anyway, with how much attention I plan on giving you." I shake my head, knowing this is something he will absolutely follow through on. "You have nothing to worry about with Mrs. Bianchi. That woman thinks so highly of you, she will understand and trust you."

"I hope so."

"Trust me. Remember, always right."

I can't help but giggle, remembering our conversation at breakfast.

We agree that since I won't be available next weekend, Luke should stay in London as originally planned. I'll miss him, but I'm looking forward to spending time with Amelia. Besides, his absence will buy me some time to decide how to tell everyone I'm dating him.

———

I arrive home with a few hours to spare before Grant returns Amelia. I start a load of laundry and straighten up the house. Then it's time to make some phone calls. I dial Emily first, anticipating she will be the least troubled by the latest development in my love life.

"Hello beautiful."

"Hi Em. You have a minute."

"I just pulled up to the gym. What's up?"

"How was your date Friday?" I ask.

"Boring. He talked about his job and his mom most of the night. At one point he even brought up his ex-girlfriend. I don't have time to teach someone proper dating etiquette. I need someone who needs less training."

I laugh. "I'm not sure you should need to train anyone. Sounds like he just wasn't the right guy for you."

"I guess. How was your weekend? How many pints did you eat?" My ice cream consumption is well known and has become Emily's measure of how well I'm doing.

"None," I say proudly.

"None? What did you do?"

"I took a last-minute trip to San Francisco."

"That doesn't sound anything like you. Who talked you into that?"

"Luke." I scrunch my face, waiting for her reaction.

"What?" Emily practically screams into the phone. "I need all the details, now."

I tell her about the weekend, excluding the more intimate details.

"I can't believe you went to see Maroon 5 without me." She pretends to pout. She is usually my concert companion.

"I promise my next concert is with you."

"All right," she says, still using her sulky voice. "I'm proud of you. You need a little adventure in your life."

"This is why I called you first. I knew you'd be happy for me."

"Vivien will be concerned, but she'll be happy too."

"Yeah, I know. I'm more nervous about my mom's reaction," I admit.

"This may not be what you want to hear, but your mom knows Luke more than we do, and she doesn't take crap from any man. I would trust her opinion."

"I know. That's why I'm afraid."

"You won't know until you talk to her."

"Thanks. You're a good friend, Emily."

"I try. Good luck."

I knew talking to her first was a good idea. I dial Vivien, feeling a bit more confident.

"Hey girl," she answers.

"Hey, I've got some news to share."

"Good news or bad news?" Vivien always likes to mentally prepare.

"Good." I hope she agrees.

"What's going on?"

"The condensed version is, Luke showed up at my work and we talked. He convinced me to join him in San Francisco for the weekend. I admit the weekend was up and down, but in the end we decided to try dating again."

Vivien doesn't say anything.

Her silence makes me uncomfortable. I want to ease her concern. "I wouldn't get involved with him again if I didn't think he was different."

She sighs. "When you said good news, this wasn't at all what I was expecting. You sound happy, so I'm happy for you."

"You sound ecstatic," I say sarcastically.

"Sorry. You know I'm a worrier. I don't want to see you get hurt again." My heart aches. I sometimes forget that my divorce didn't just affect me. It caused those who love me to worry and hurt too.

"I know, and that's why I love you. I'm going into this thing with Luke with caution."

"I'm sure you are."

I can't think of anything to say right now to ease her mind, so I change the subject. "Did you hear about Emily's date?"

We talk for a few more minutes before Vivien has to go. I feel good about ending our conversation on a lighter note. I ready myself to make the most difficult call. I dial her house phone instead of her cell, half hoping she isn't home.

My mom answers after the second ring. "Hello?"

"Hi, Mom." I don't want my nervousness to alarm her, so I try to sound as normal as possible.

"Hey, honey."

"Are you busy? Do you have a minute?"

"I'm cleaning out the fridge. Talking with you will be a good distraction."

"I went to San Francisco this weekend."

"That's great. Wait, you didn't tell me you were going away."

"It was kind of a last-minute trip." I cringe, knowing I'm stalling.

"How fun. With Emily?"

"Not with Emily." I twist my mouth.

"Vivien?" I can hear the apprehension in her voice.

"Not Vivien either."

My mother sighs. "Luke." It's not a question.

"Yeah, with Luke."

"How did it go?" she asks cautiously.

"Honestly, it was up and down, but we cleared up a lot."

"Well, that's good."

"There's more."

"Oh, I'm sure there is."

"We decided to try dating again." My mother is silent long enough to make me uncomfortable. "Mom, are you going to say anything?"

"Jessica, you're an adult and can do what you want. You don't need my permission." Her voice is gentle.

"I'm not asking for your permission, but I thought you may have some feelings to share."

"It doesn't matter what I think. It matters what you think."

"Mom," I complain.

"Jessica." My mom mimics my tone.

"Don't do that. I didn't jump into this easily, and I could use some support."

"You know I always support you."

"Mom, I'm serious." I pause before asking a question I'm dreading her answer to. "You think I'm making a mistake, don't you?"

"Ugh…" She sighs again. "I've seen you at your best and your worst. I've seen you go through immense joy and awful heartbreak."

"This year has been difficult for everyone."

"I'm not talking about this year. I'm talking about with Luke."

"Oh," I whisper.

"I always liked Luke. He brought out some great qualities in you and made you shine even brighter. Relationships like that are rare. I also remember how crushed you were when he left."

"That was a long time ago. I can accept that he was young and immature."

"It was, and he was."

"And I got over it. I married Grant and had Amelia…"

"Yes, and you've had a good life. But you and I both know you never had the feelings for Grant that you had for Luke."

I frown even though she can't see me.

"I'm not saying you didn't love Grant, but you know I'm right. It was never quite the same."

"I don't think it's fair to compare the two."

"Maybe not. Anyway, I liked Luke. I liked the way you used to light up when you were with him. I liked that he got you to open up and try new things, all while encouraging you to be you. I have no idea what type of man he has grown up to be, but if he still affects you the way he used to, well, I don't imagine you could stay away from him even if you tried. I'm only worried about what happens if it doesn't work out."

"Me too," I admit.

"I'm not going to tell you to be careful, because that wouldn't be very good advice. So…have fun."

"That's your advice. Have fun?" I can't help but giggle.

"Yep. I love you, but sometimes you think the fun out of things."

"I'll try," I promise her.

"And tell Luke, if he pulls any bullshit antics this time, I will track him down."

I laugh again. "I'll give him your scary warning. Mom, I'm worried about something else."

"What's that?"

"What about Amelia? I feel guilty enough about her not living with both Grant and myself."

"And?"

"Well, I mean, introducing another man into her life…I don't want to upset her any more than I already have."

"Oh, sweetie. You worry too much. Amelia will be fine. Besides, I'm guessing you don't have any immediate plans to introduce her to Luke anyway."

"No, not yet."

"I'm going to ask you to do yourself a favor."

"What?"

"Take everything one step at a time. Worry about one stage at a time. You'll find things have a way of falling into place when it's meant to be."

I agree with her, but it's easier said than done. "I don't know if I can do that. I don't like to be caught off guard."

"Life is like that, always full of surprises. I can't make you not worry about things. I never have been able to. I simply want to caution you to not waste your life worrying about the maybes of tomorrow. Enjoy the realities of today."

"Wow, you've definitely been talking to your sister more, haven't you?" I laugh.

She laughs too. I've always loved her laugh. It is everything a mom laugh should be, full of love and life. "She is one of the happiest people I know, so maybe she's not so crazy after all."

"Thanks, Mom. I love you." I do feel better after talking to her.

"I love you too, sweetie. Keep me posted."

"I will. Bye."

"Bye."

Grant brings Amelia home a few minutes after I hang up with my mom. Amelia and I spend the evening catching up and getting ready for the week. After I put her to bed, I watch the news. I try to follow my mom's advice and not worry about the concerns that remain.

The week goes by quickly. I still haven't told anyone at work about Luke by the time Friday rolls around. I feel guilty not telling Linda. She can sense something is off, but she doesn't pry after I assure her there is nothing to be concerned about.

I spend the weekend with Amelia and my mom. I missed them both last weekend, and the family time reenergizes me. I sneak in a couple of late-night phone calls with Luke after Amelia is asleep.

Butterflies swirl in my stomach Monday morning. I need to tell people at work about Luke and me.

"Good morning." Linda sounds extra chipper this morning when I enter the office.

"Good morning. Sounds like you had a good weekend."

"I did. My daughter got engaged." Linda is beaming.

"Oh Linda. That's wonderful news. I know you've always liked her boyfriend."

"Yeah. He's a good guy. They're a good match. He asked us last month for our blessing. It's been hard to keep such a big secret."

Her innocent comment makes me feel guilty. "Did they set a date?" I ask.

"No, but they are thinking sometime next summer."

"How exciting. If she has any interest in getting married here, I'm sure Mrs. Bianchi would give her a good deal."

"I'll mention it to her. All she said is that she wants it to be outdoors. I hope she doesn't plan on incorporating all her animals." We both laugh. "How was your weekend?"

"It was good. Not as eventful as yours though. I took Amelia to the apple farms up in Oak Glen."

"I've never made it up there. How was it?" she asks.

"It was good. Apple cider, apple doughnuts, apple pie...lots of apples. After making a cobbler with the fruit we picked, I don't think I'll be eating anything apple for a while."

Linda laughs. "I don't blame you. How do you feel about blueberries? I brought muffins."

"I think my relationship with blueberries is in good standing. Speaking of relationships—"

Linda's phone rings, and she holds up a finger. "Hold that thought. Good morning, Mrs. Bianchi...Yes, I have the papers right here. I can bring them to you now if you'd like...Great. I'll be right there...Sure. I will tell her...Bye." Linda hangs up and says, "Mrs. Bianchi would like to meet with you around eleven to go over the new cost of sales numbers."

"Got it. I better go review them one last time." I'll tell Linda later about Luke.

The rest of the day flies by. I'm surprised when Linda says goodbye at five o'clock. I cringe that I've let another day pass without telling her or anyone about Luke. I need to before he returns.

I make it into work the next morning a little late due to Amelia forgetting her lunch on the kitchen counter. She protested so much when I told her to buy lunch I decided it wasn't a battle worth fighting. I drove back home to retrieve her bag and had to walk it into the school office when I returned with it.

I hate being late. By the time I'm finally seated at my desk, I'm unsettled. I have a missed phone call from Mrs. Bianchi. I dial her extension immediately.

"Good morning. Sorry I missed your call. What can I do for you?"

"Good morning. Were you able to make the adjustments we discussed yesterday?"

"I did. Would you like to see the updated numbers?"

"I would. Are you available around eleven?"

"I can be." I will need to move a meeting I have scheduled with Ryan, but that shouldn't be a problem.

"I have brainstorming sessions scheduled with the marketing and sales departments in the afternoon, so if you can, that would be great."

"Not a problem. I'll see you at eleven."

"Great." She hangs up.

I email Ryan, and he responds that rescheduling for this afternoon is fine. A little before eleven, I grab a cup of tea from the kitchen and head to Mrs. Bianchi's office. We review the new numbers and are both pleased with the results. We're finishing up when her cell chimes, indicating she has an incoming call.

"Hello Aaron…Yes, we're still on for lunch today. Hey, I'm sitting here with Jessica. Do you mind if I invite her to come along?" Mrs. Bianchi pauses to listen. "Sounds good…I will."

"I know it's short notice, but can you join us for lunch today?" Mrs. Bianchi asks after ending her call.

I doubt Aaron will say anything about Luke and me. He's very professional, and I can't picture him bringing it up if I don't.

"Sure."

"He wants to meet at another winery to scope out the competition. Ryan is also coming along."

Ryan has been acting weird toward me ever since the investor dinner. We agreed to be friends, but his behavior over the past week has led me to believe otherwise. He hasn't done anything inappropriate, but a woman can sense these things. The little looks he gives me, him coming by my office when a simple email would suffice, the way he seems to be searching for reasons to interact with me. Our meeting today was his idea, and I'm not sure it's completely necessary. My warning alarms are ringing.

Mrs. Bianchi pulls her keys from a desk drawer and stands. "Oh, Luke just flew back into town, so he's joining us too."

And just like that, I panic.

Chapter 14

Mrs. Bianchi and Ryan talk the entire way to lunch. I have no idea what they're discussing though because all I can think about is how to tell them I'm dating the investor we're meeting for lunch. I'm mad at myself for not saying anything last week, when I could have found a way to bring it up naturally. I think about texting Luke, but Ryan keeps looking back at me intently, like he's trying to figure something out. Better to not draw any additional attention to myself by frantically typing out a message to Luke. Besides what would I say to him? He was very clear that he didn't want our relationship to be a secret at work. The fact that I've had over a week to tell everyone and haven't isn't going to go over well with him. This is a conversation that should happen in person.

We arrive at the winery before Luke and Aaron. Mrs. Bianchi lets the hostess know there will be five of us dining today, and she quickly shows us to a table near the back of the restaurant. We take our seats. I'm about to blurt out something along the lines of "I'm dating Luke," when the waitress arrives and asks for our drink order. Mrs. Bianchi orders a bottle of pinot grigio and a bottle of sangiovese. After the waitress leaves, I'm about to force the words out when Mrs. Bianchi rises.

"Aaron, Luke, over here." She waves them over enthusiastically.

Luke beams when he sees me. I smile back, but as he approaches, panic returns. I stick out my hand when he is still several steps away from the table.

"So nice to see you both again." My voice comes out in a pitch higher than normal.

Luke stares at my outstretched hand. The look of terror on my face tells him all he needs to know. His demeanor changes in an instant. His handshake is firm, and the expression in his eyes tells me how much he dislikes the position I've put him in.

Aaron glances between Luke and me. "Hello, Jessica."

We sit, and I bury my face in a menu.

To say that lunch is uncomfortable is an understatement. Luke avoids all conversation or eye contact with me. I do notice he runs his hands through his hair several times, a sure sign that he's frustrated.

I try to eat the salad I ordered, but my stomach indicates it is going to reject anything I try to put in it in a violent way. I sip my ice water instead. The rest of the table is finishing up their lunches when I excuse myself to the restroom.

I can't splash water on my face because of my makeup, so I have to settle for some deep breaths and a cool paper towel on the back of my neck. I send Luke a text saying I'm sorry and that I promise to fix everything.

When I return to the table, they are still engaged in a conversation about the winemaking process. It's subtle, and the others don't notice, but Luke's mood has shifted. He was tense and uncomfortable before, but now he's angry. The waitress returns to see if anyone would like dessert or coffee. Thankfully everyone declines. Luke still won't look at me, and he keeps his attention on the others.

Aaron asks Mrs. Bianchi a question about sales, and Ryan uses the break to lean over to me.

"Are you all right?" he whispers.

"Yeah," I mutter. I look at Luke. He is stretching his neck.

Ryan pats my arm before reengaging in the conversation. Luke glares at me for a split second, then replaces the expression with one more appropriate for a business lunch.

After several excruciating minutes, the waitress returns with the bill.

"I got it this time." Luke smiles at Mrs. Bianchi. The smile he gives her is genuine, but he has to unclench his hand to pick it up. This is bad.

Luke pays in cash, so we don't have to wait for the waitress to return. We walk to the parking lot together, where we say our goodbyes. Luke shakes Mrs. Bianchi's hand first. They laugh and promise to grab a drink next time he is in town. He shakes Ryan's hand next. Ryan flinches slightly, indicating Luke has used a little extra strength.

I extend my hand to him once again. I can't stop it from shaking. He shakes it and says goodbye, his face and voice devoid of emotion. He walks away without any indication of wanting to talk to me. He ignores the texts I send to him during the car ride back to the winery, and I fight back tears.

Back at the winery, I thank Mrs. Bianchi for inviting me to lunch. Ryan reminds me about our meeting later before I head back to my office. The door is locked, meaning Linda must be elsewhere. I punch in my code and enter.

When I open the door to my private office, I'm startled by the sight of Luke sitting in my desk chair. Even though he doesn't look happy, I'm glad to see him. I would rather have him mad at me than ignore me.

"Where's Linda?" This conversation may be unpleasant, and I don't want any witnesses.

"She mentioned she had to leave early and you knew about it." Luke sounds calm, but I can tell he's upset. "I thought you said you and Ryan were just friends."

"We are."

"Hm."

"I don't know what you're implying, but there is nothing going on with Ryan."

"Then explain to me why I was just at a lunch with my girl-friend, who is apparently keeping our relationship a secret even after I told her I wasn't interested in doing that, and another man tells me, my best friend, and your boss that things are progressing between you two?"

"What?" I screech. I'm shocked and saddened that Ryan would say something like that, especially at a business func-tion. "Nothing is progressing between us."

Luke cuts me off by raising his hand. "He even told us how you two went on a date not too long ago." I sense Luke's effort to suppress his anger. "I don't know what exactly went on between you two, but I don't like being caught off guard."

"Let me explain."

"Please do."

"I went to dinner with Ryan months ago, before I even saw you at the reunion. It was just dinner, but even that didn't feel right. I thought I had been clear with Ryan. I told him we were better as friends. He agreed, and I thought we were both on the same page, but him bringing it up today in front of you and Mrs. Bianchi means I clearly need to have another talk with him."

Luke uncrosses his arms and relaxes his shoulders slightly.

"The dinner was unimportant, and I knew you already didn't like Ryan, so I didn't bother to mention it. I'm sorry you found out that way. I should've told you."

"Why didn't you tell them we're dating?"

I squeeze my eyes shut. "I was going to, I am going to. I just haven't been able to find the right time to do it."

Luke sighs and leans back in the chair.

He doesn't have to say anything. I know what I need to do. I walk around to the other side of my desk, reach across him, and pick up the phone. I dial Mrs. Bianchi's extension, hoping to catch her before her next meeting begins. She answers on the third ring.

"Hello."

"Do you have a minute?"

"A quick one, just waiting for Monica."

"I need to tell you something, Mrs. Bianchi." I take a deep breath. "I messed up earlier, because I didn't know how to tell you. I didn't want you to think differently of me or that I was acting unprofessionally, but I have recently started dating Luke."

"I guess my husband was correct. He thought he noticed sparks between you two."

"Truth is, I knew him in high school, and we decided to try a relationship again. I promise I won't let it affect my job in any way." I bite my lip.

"Luke is not an employee of the winery, and you're both adults, so I don't see any problem with it."

"Thank you." I relax.

"While we're on the subject though, Ryan *is* my employee, and he had some interesting things to say at lunch today. Since you're dating Luke now, I suppose it doesn't matter so much, but I would encourage you to be clear with Ryan. I've never expressly prohibited employees from dating, but it can lead to hurt feelings and uncomfortable interactions."

"I understand. I'll clear things up with him."

"Sounds good. Oh, and Jessica, I hope Luke makes you happy."

"He does."

I hang up. Luke pulls me down into his lap.

"Thank you." He buries his face in my neck.

"I should've done it before."

"Yes, but then we wouldn't have the opportunity to have makeup sex in your office."

"Luke…" I say his name in a warning tone, but his lips are already pressed against my neck. "Not fair. You know that's my weakness."

"I never said I play fair."

He pushes me up from his lap, leans down, and places his hands on the back of my knees. He glides up the back of my legs and under my skirt until he reaches his destination. He squeezes my ass before hooking his fingers around the top edge of my panties. He peers up at me, and I know I should tell him we can't do this. Problem is, I want to.

His warm hands skim my legs as he pulls my underwear down, and it makes me shiver. I grab his shoulder as I step out of them, and he kisses my arm. When he stands and takes my face in his hands, I hold my breath.

He presses his soft lips to mine and slides his tongue past them.

"You taste good," I murmur. He moves his hands into my hair and kisses me harder. Our mouths grow eager as they battle for more. I bite his bottom lip, and he groans.

In one motion he drops his hands to my waist and lifts me onto the desk. He sits in front of me and pulls me to the edge, roughly spreading my legs apart and placing my heels on the armrests.

"In case you forgot, let me remind you how I make you feel." He licks his lips, and I gasp. He buries his face between my legs, and everything else fades away. After only a few minutes, my legs are shaking.

"I want you inside me," I breathe out.

He stands up and kicks the chair back, then reaches in his pocket and retrieves a condom. He quickly undresses and gets ready to remind me some more.

He crashes into me. First with his mouth and then with his body. I'm so distracted by the intensity of his kiss, I'm caught off guard when he swiftly enters me. I gasp. The sound seems to turn him on even more because he mumbles something against my mouth and pushes into me harder. The more I moan, the faster and harder he thrusts. I remember we're in my office and I try to be quieter. The thought makes my heart race, and a rush of adrenaline courses through me. The idea that we're breaking a rule, that we could be caught, is taking this encounter to another level.

"Luke. I want you to make me come on this desk," I whisper in his ear before taking the lobe in my mouth and sucking.

"Absolutely." He reaches between us and rubs in small circles. The waves of my orgasm ripple through me. I cry out louder than I mean to, and he tenses, releases, and crumples against me.

We stay this way for a couple of minutes, until Luke's legs start to weaken. He kisses me on the forehead before pulling out of me. I smile as I hop off the desk.

"I don't want anyone else to ever make you smile like that."

"No one does." I pick up my panties and put them on.

"I missed you." He pulls his pants back on.

"I missed you too."

"You don't understand. I'm not sure I've ever missed anyone while I've been away on a business trip."

"That's a good thing, right?"

"Yeah, it's a good thing." He grabs my hand and gently places a kiss on it.

I canceled my afternoon meeting with Ryan yesterday. I wasn't in the right frame of mind after Luke left. But I don't want a repeat of yesterday's lunch, so I need to talk to Ryan today. Luke offered to handle it for me, but his wicked smile as he said it let me know he would not handle the situation with compassion.

I knock on the door to the winemaker's office.

"Come in," Ryan yells from inside.

I enter, and he smiles at me from a desk strewn with papers, a stark contrast to my organized office. "Got a minute?"

"Sure." He motions for me to sit in the chair across from him.

"I'm not here to make you feel bad, but I heard you told the others at lunch yesterday about our date. I don't want any misunderstandings between us. I thought we agreed we're just friends."

"Yes, we are. I'm sorry. I shouldn't have said anything."

"Why did you say anything at all? It was a dinner date. It happened ages ago." I let out a frustrated sigh. "I'm not mad. I just want to know what's going on."

"Okay. I would love to be more than your friend. I'm sure that's not a big surprise to you. But I know you don't feel the same way about me, and that's fine."

"You're a good man, and you deserve a good woman. Unfortunately, that woman isn't me. I care about you, Ryan, just not in that way."

"I care about you too." Ryan sighs. "That's why I brought it up. One of the investors has had his eye on you from the beginning. I've seen the way he looks at you. At lunch yesterday, he watched as you walked away from the table. He watched you like you're something that belongs to him. I felt I needed to protect you."

"I have to tell you something." I fidget in my seat. This is going to be harder than I thought.

He pales and shrinks back in the chair as he realizes what I'm not telling him. "Come on…you slept with that guy?"

"It's not like that."

Ryan shakes his head. "Oh, so you think you're special to him? I really thought you were smarter than that."

"I'm going to give you a pass on that comment." I look Ryan directly in the eye. "You don't understand the situation."

"Oh, I think I do. What is it? His money? His looks? What exactly is it you're attracted to? Because it certainly isn't kindness or someone treating you with respect."

"That's enough," I warn.

"What the hell, Jessica? You go from one cheater's bed to another? Because we both know that's how this ends, right?" He's flushed with anger.

I stand and move toward the door. "You're out of line, and you're making a lot of assumptions concerning something you know nothing about." I slam the door as I leave.

I walk across the property and back to my office, the whole time praying he's wrong.

Chapter 15

For the first time since Grant and I split, I'm not dreading a weekend without Amelia. I'll still miss her terribly, but I'm excited Luke will be spending the weekend at my house. His apartment is beautiful, but my house is comfortable and homey. I can't envision living in an apartment like Luke's full time. I'm also eager to see how we interact as a couple under more normal, ordinary circumstances.

My blowup with Ryan left me frazzled for the next couple of days. When I told Luke about it, he was ready to come to the winery and straighten Ryan out. I assured him that wasn't necessary. Ryan and I have been avoiding each other, and that works for me.

When I told Linda about Luke, she didn't seem surprised. She said she could tell something was different and suspected I had begun dating someone. She was surprised to learn about my past with Luke and all the drama. I love Linda and consider her a friend, but I am her boss too. I probably overshare, so this time I left out some of the more graphic details from the past few weeks.

I glance at the clock and see it's already four. "Linda, why don't you start your weekend early?"

"Are you sure?"

"Yeah, it's been a long week. Get out of here."

"Thanks. Have a nice weekend with Luke. Can't wait to hear all about it." She turns off her computer and gathers her belongings.

"You too," I say right as I hear the office door close. She told me earlier she's having neighbors over for dinner tonight, so I don't take her speedy departure personally.

I'm eager to go home and get ready for Luke's arrival. Mrs. Bianchi doesn't mandate exact times we have to be at work. As long as we don't abuse her generosity and leave at noon every day, we're allowed some leeway to come and go as we please.

I make it home with time to shower and get dinner started. I'm not the type to always cook dinner, but with Luke's travel schedule, I assume he eats out often. If he can spoil me with private plane rides and fancy clothes, I want to treat him in my own way. Tonight he's getting chicken parmesan and homemade brownies.

Luke rings my doorbell as I'm sticking pans in the oven. I know it's him, but I peer through the peephole anyway. He looks tired but peaceful. His relaxed demeanor softens his features and makes him appear more boyish, more like the Luke I remember from high school. When I open the door and see the outline of his biceps through his T-shirt, I'm reminded he is in no way a boy.

He smiles and hands me a bouquet of stargazer lilies. They've been my favorite since my mom started buying them for me when I was ten. She told me every girl should receive flowers, and she shouldn't have to wait for a boy to give them to her. To this day we send each other flowers several times a year. I'm looking forward to carrying on the tradition with Amelia once she's a little older.

"I pictured you using a fancy suitcase these days." I point to the duffel bag slung over his shoulder.

He kisses me on the cheek as he steps through the doorway. "I was so used to carrying around my baseball stuff in a bag, I guess I never moved on. Some habits are hard to break."

"Do you still play?" I realize I don't know if he completely gave up the game he loved so much at one time in his life.

"Sometimes with the kids at the center. I played on a softball league a while back, but then I got too busy."

"Well, maybe you'll have a son or daughter to play with someday." I cringe as the words come out of my mouth.

Luke sets his bag down by the bottom of my staircase and steps toward me. "I don't want kids, but I do want to practice with you." He presses his lips against mine.

I'm breathless and a little dazed when he releases me. This is the first time I've heard him say he doesn't want children. A buzzing sound from the kitchen interrupts my swirling thoughts before I can ask him to elaborate.

"I smell chocolate." he grins at me.

"Brownies."

"My favorite." He plants another kiss on my lips before heading toward the kitchen.

I straighten up the kitchen while Luke tells me about London and the tech company he was visiting. When dinner is ready, I plate the food and Luke opens a bottle of wine.

"I thought you might enjoy a home-cooked meal after being gone."

"It smells great."

"Do you like traveling so much?" I carry our plates to the dining table.

"I do. Or I used to. I enjoy seeing new places and meeting people, but it's nice to be home too. My schedule has made it difficult to do some of the other things I enjoy." Luke sets a glass of wine in front of me before sitting.

"When did you stop playing baseball? Did you play after college?" I place a bite of chicken in my mouth.

"I played four years at Florida State. I had offers to play in the minors, but I was burnt out. Knew I wasn't going pro, so I decided to get my career started."

"Did you know this is what you wanted to do?" "At twenty-two, I didn't have a clue what I was going to do with a business degree. I lucked out when a teammate's dad basically took me under his wing and taught me about venture capital. He saw I was a hard worker on the field and took a chance I might do the same at his company. I still remember the first meeting I got to sit in on. It was a rush, these really smart people attempting to get deals worked out. The next morning I got into the office before everyone. I stayed that night until I could barely see straight. I was hungry to learn as much as I could. I continued to do that until one day, they called me in to participate in a pitch meeting. I was nervous, but I listened and tried to ask meaningful questions. They said I was a natural and began to give me more projects. I met Aaron a couple of years later at a conference in Miami, and we instantly clicked. Within a year I moved to San Francisco to launch AL Investments with him."

"It's really not fair that you're good at everything you do," I tease.

"Not true. I'm good at things I'm determined to be good at. Speaking of being good at things, what about your photography?"

"No, I haven't had time for that in years."

"Well, good thing I'm back."

"Why? Are you going to pose for me?" I snicker at the thought.

"No, but I am going to make sure you find time to do things that make you happy."

After dinner, Luke ignores my protests and insists on helping me clean up the kitchen. When we are done, he thanks me again for dinner and pours me another glass of merlot. I take out the trash, and when I return, Luke is no longer in the kitchen. He's in the backyard, walking around the pool, sipping his glass of wine. I pick up my glass and join him outside.

"Nice yard. I do miss having one of these."

"Yeah, it's nice to have a mini escape back here. Amelia and I come out here a lot on weekends."

Luke sits on the cushioned loveseat and pats the space next to him. I ignite the fire table before sitting next to him. Despite its potential danger, fire is soothing to be around. Luke is fire.

He is uncharacteristically quiet, and it's making him hard to read. He gazes at the stars. I consider asking him what he's thinking about, but it's so cliché. People will tell you what they're thinking if they want to. Asking is annoying. Grant used to often ask me what I was feeling. Reflecting on it now, I don't know that he ever really cared about the answer.

We sit this way for what seems like a long time. My mind drifts to other things: work, Amelia, what I want to make for dinner next week. Spending time with Luke is comfortable and easy.

"This really is a nice house."

"Thank you."

"I have to admit I was a little uneasy with the idea of being in the house where you had a life with Grant once, but I can see why you're happy here. I don't see him anywhere."

"Well, I should hope not, since he's never lived here."

"Oh, I assumed…" Luke tips his head to one side.

"I moved out when I found out about Grant's cheating. Grant is still in our old place, but it's up for sale. I knew I wouldn't be able to start over in that house. Too many memories." I take a gulp of wine. I don't enjoy speaking about Grant, especially with Luke.

The silence returns, and although I wouldn't say it's uncomfortable, I wish Grant had not been brought up at all.

"Want to go in the spa?" I ask after a few minutes.

Luke smiles at me. "Yeah."

I shiver in the best way possible.

By the time I return to the backyard after changing into my swimsuit and fetching towels, Luke is already there. He happened to pack a pair of board shorts, but I wouldn't have minded if he hadn't. Luke sticks his foot into the water as I lay the towels on one of the lounge chairs nearby.

"It's warming up. It's probably warm enough to—" He stops talking.

"What?" I'm not usually self-conscious in a bathing suit, at least not to this extent, but Luke studies me with such intensity, I feel naked.

"Not sorry I'm staring. I haven't seen you in a bikini in over ten years. You look even better than I remembered."

"Luke, you've seen me in less," I remind him as heat rises in my cheeks.

"Yeah, but there's still something about a woman in a bikini. No, I take that back, there's something about you in one."

I shake my head and step into the spa. Luke follows me in.

We sit across from each other as steam rises off the water. I rub my neck and adjust my ponytail.

"Can I ask you something?" Luke leans back with his arms spread wide.

"Of course." I glance away, trying to escape the intensity of his eyes on me.

"Do you get this nervous with all men or only me?"

"Only you." I move my hands from my hair to my lap to my sides. I can't seem to find a comfortable resting place.

"Why?"

"Other men don't treat me the way you do."

"How so?"

"Well, the things you say to me…the compliments…the way you look at me."

"How do I look at you?"

"You know."

"Yeah, I know, but I want to hear you say it." His voice is low, raspy.

"You look at me like I'm the only woman in the room." I swallow hard. "Like you wish there was no one else there."

"Well, that's a mild way to put it." He moves toward me, places his hands on my hips, and stands between my legs. "We're alone right now."

"We are," I whisper, and my heartbeat quickens.

"Do you want to know how I think I look at you?"

I resist the urge to pull him to me. I mean to answer yes, but no words come out.

"I look at you how you deserve to be looked at. I look at you like I'm lucky to have your attention." He places a slow, soft kiss on my lips. "I look at you like you're the only woman who's ever truly mattered."

I don't resist this time. I grab the back of his neck and pull his mouth to mine. Our tongues collide and dance around each other. His hands make quick work of removing the top of my bathing suit. I moan when he squeezes my exposed nipples.

We freeze as a door opens and laughter invades the peacefulness of the night. It takes me a couple of seconds to register that it's my neighbors, heading outside with their guests. By the loudness of the voices, it seems they have chosen to sit at their patio table, which is directly on the other side of my block wall.

Luke puts a finger up to my lips. He leans down and kisses and sucks on my neck. I lean my head back and concentrate on remaining quiet.

With my help, he slides my bottoms off. He reaches between my legs and strokes me. I'm conflicted. I don't want to put on a show for my neighbors, but I also don't want him to stop.

"We have an unexpected audience," he whispers. "I don't care if they hear or not, but I am going to make you come with them sitting on the other side of that fence."

"Luke—"

He touches my lips, then lifts one of my breasts above the water. He takes it in his mouth as he plunges his fingers inside me. He rubs me with his thumb while pumping his fingers in and out. His tongue swirls and caresses my sensitive skin. I feel my orgasm building. I worry I won't be able to stay quiet enough. I whimper, and he quickly covers my mouth with his, swallowing every sound I make as I pulsate around his fingers.

"It's okay to keep going," I say. I know he stopped because he didn't bring a condom outside. I also know from some difficult but necessary phone conversations we've had that he's practiced safe sex and has been tested on a regular basis. I assured him I too was tested after I found out about the affair.

"Are you sure?"

"Yeah."

"What about…?"

"Not a time when I can get pregnant."

He removes his shorts and pushes inside me. The water increases the friction, and I feel more filled than I usually do. He senses this and moves slowly. It's like I can feel every inch of him inside me. He looks into my eyes as he thrusts. It's the most erotic sexual experience I've ever had, even with people sitting only several feet away—or maybe because of them. Luke gives me one last deep kiss before letting go.

Chapter 16

We don't open our eyes until after eight o'clock. I slept all night without waking once. I can't remember the last time that happened. Wait, yes I do. It was in Luke's apartment, that second night. He obviously knows how to wear me out.

While Luke answers emails, I slip out of bed and go downstairs. If I don't get up now, we'll end up spending all day in bed. While not a completely horrible option, I want to spend time together as a typical couple. We already know we're compatible in the bedroom. I want to see how we interact during a regular day, although I suspect that nothing he does is ordinary.

He enters the kitchen as I'm pouring our drinks, coffee for him and a chai tea latte for me. He is wearing pajama bottoms, and his hair sticks up in weird directions. Even with messy hair, Luke exudes a sexy vibe. I like seeing his casual side. It's less intimidating than the suit and tie I often see him in. He reminds me of the boy I used to do my homework with.

I snicker at the sight of him looking disheveled.

"What?" Luke wears a fake frown. He's too confident to be self-conscious.

"Oh, nothing. I figured out how to deal with you in business meetings from now on." I sip my tea.

"Oh yeah?" His eyes sparkle.

"From now on, any time I'm intimidated by you, I'm going to picture you like this, standing in my kitchen, looking like your mom made you get out of bed to go to school."

"Hm," he mumbles and drinks his coffee. "Would you like to know how I picture you during our business meetings?" He has such a wicked grin on his face, I blush instantly.

"No," I practically yell at him. "Never mind, you win. I'll stay intimidated."

He laughs. "What's the plan?"

"No plan. We could go wine tasting or hiking or to the movies. I was thinking something low-key today."

"Maybe a drive down to Pacific Beach? We could have lunch and walk around."

"That sounds perfect."

"You sure? I'm happy to do whatever. I was only thinking I haven't been there in a long time."

"Me neither. Really, it's perfect."

An hour later, we're dressed and ready. We bring chairs and a blanket in case we want to sit on the sand. Even though it is unseasonably warm in Temecula today, it will be colder by the water. We'll be comfortable as long as it's not too windy, otherwise it will probably be too chilly to sit on the sand.

We stop for breakfast at Penfold's Café. It's my favorite place for breakfast. My stomach growls when we enter the restaurant and are met by the scent of fresh-baked cinnamon rolls. It's not a fancy place, but the food is good, and the people are friendly. As much fun as fancy parties and trips to San Francisco are, this is really more my style.

I order the blueberry pancakes. Luke goes with a healthier option of eggs and turkey sausage. We both read sections of a newspaper left behind by a previous patron. I notice other couples around the restaurant, many of them older, who have settled into their own morning rituals. I wonder if this is something Luke and I will do again. The thought makes me smile. It's a perfect way to start a casual Saturday.

Luke drives, and I'm grateful for the opportunity to enjoy the scenery. I love daydreaming and watching the khaki colored hillsides pass by. My ten-minute work commute is too short to let my mind wander like this.

"Tell me something you've done during the past ten years that I don't know about," Luke says, startling me from my meandering thoughts.

From anyone else, I may have considered that question intrusive and forced, but I know he's actually interested. "Let me think. Oh, I saw my father a few years ago."

"You did?" Luke doesn't hide his surprise and glances over at me.

"He lives in Wyoming now. It was about as eventful and memorable as you would expect. He couldn't give me an explanation as to why he hadn't made any effort to see me over the years."

"I'm sorry. If it makes you feel any better, sometimes having a parent around isn't necessarily better."

He's referring to his relationship with his father, which was strained in high school. He pushed Luke in baseball—too hard, many would argue. Luke turned into a great athlete, but their relationship suffered. It's disappointing to hear that things haven't gotten better between them.

"How are your parents?" I regret I haven't asked before now.

"Mom passed away a couple of years ago from a rare form of liver cancer. By the time they found it…it was quick. Dad is drinking his way to join her."

"I'm so sorry Luke." I cringe, remembering the comment I made earlier about his mom getting him out of bed. "Your mom was always so kind to me."

"Yeah, she always liked you. She was pretty pissed at me after I broke up with you."

"But I bet your dad was thrilled."

"It wasn't personal. He didn't like anything or anyone that distracted me from baseball. And you are definitely distracting." He exits the freeway.

When we arrive in Pacific Beach, we drive around for twenty minutes, taking it all in. We used to come here sometimes during our high school years. Like everything else from our youth, things look different, but they evoke familiar feelings.

"Remember when we had dinner there?" I ask when we pass a restaurant I recognize.

"Weren't Karen and Matt with us that night?"

"Oh, that's right! We tried to set them up." I giggle at our failed matchmaker attempts.

"Matt kept making really inappropriate jokes, trying to get Karen to laugh."

"She was convinced he was trying to offend her on purpose."

"I promise you he wasn't. Matt's game was truly that bad."

"Do you keep in touch with Matt? I saw him at the reunion and met his wife."

"We text sometimes, but before the reunion I hadn't seen him in probably three years. He's married with a couple of kids. We don't have that much in common."

Luke parks and we get out of the car. The hours pass quickly as we peer in the storefront windows and pause to watch street performers. We pass a group of boisterous teens and sarcastically comment there is absolutely no way we were ever that annoying.

We stop for lunch at a little pizza place.

"I haven't had pizza in forever," Luke remarks as he reads the menu.

"We can go somewhere else."

"No way. I love pizza. I've missed it."

"Dating me may prove damaging to your physique." I'm only half joking.

"Are you only dating me for my body?" Luke raises his eyebrows at me over the top of his menu.

"Maybe," I tease. "I just don't want to be responsible for ruining your hard work."

"I'm glad you're taking such an active interest in my body." Luke laughs when I cover my face with my menu. "I'll be fine. Besides, I'm pretty sure it would upset me if you stopped paying attention to it." He winks before turning his attention to the waitress who has walked up to our table.

After lunch, we walk to the end of the pier and watch the waves roll in. The wind makes the air feel cold, so he wraps his arms around me from behind to keep us both warm.

Our easy conversation causes time to pass quickly. We talk about our families more. We talk about our college days. I'm careful to not mention Grant as part of any of my memories, and he doesn't mention other women he's dated.

We're both reluctant to leave the seaside, but the sun is setting. The quiet day has produced a level of laziness in us. We agree ordering in and watching a movie is the best way to end the day.

Our Chinese food arrives as we pull up in my driveway. We take our plates of kung pao chicken, steamed vegetables, and rice to the family room.

"What do you want to watch?" I take a bite of broccoli. There is something about the salty sea air that always seems to increase my appetite. I scroll through the available movies.

"How about *It*?" Luke suggests.

"Absolutely not." I keep scrolling.

"It's a classic." He laughs.

"Nope."

"Are you really still afraid of scary movies?"

"If we watch that film, I won't sleep for several nights."

"I promise I'll protect you."

"I'm serious, Luke. I'm not watching any scary movies."

Luke raises his hands in surrender. "How about a comedy then?"

"Better." I select the newest comedy in the list and join him on the couch.

We spend the rest of the evening laughing and cuddling on the couch. It dawns on me I haven't done this in years. I feel guilty when I think about Grant, but I can't help it. Being with Luke, and experiencing things as a couple again, makes me wonder when Grant and I stopped doing a lot of things.

When it's time for bed, we go upstairs. I shower first and fall asleep while Luke is taking his. He doesn't wake me when he comes to bed, but I wake up in the middle of the night with his arms wrapped around me.

"Jessica."

I wake up to Luke standing by the bed, fully dressed in running attire. I throw the blanket over my head and try to hide.

"Good morning. Time to seize the day." Luke pries the blanket from my clenched hands.

"Are you always such a morning person?" I groan as I wait for my eyes to adjust to the sunlight filtering in through my blinds.

"Are you always so difficult in the morning?"

"Yes." I hope my answer is enough to discourage him from making me get up.

"Then I guess I'll have to be extra persuasive." He plants a kiss on my forehead before walking out of the bedroom. "I'll have tea waiting for you downstairs in fifteen minutes," he says, his voice trailing down the stairs.

I drag myself to the bathroom to prepare for a run I don't want to go on. I do want my tea though.

I dress quickly and meet Luke in the kitchen. "If you really wanted me to get up, you should've brought me some of your coffee. Where did you get it anyway? I can't seem to find it anywhere."

"It's good, right? I got it in Hawaii my last trip there. Sounds like we'll have to make a trip there to get you some."

"Are you suggesting we go to Hawaii? To buy coffee?"

"I'm suggesting we go to Hawaii so I can watch you walk around in a bikini for a few days. But if coffee is what gets you there, we'll use that as an excuse."

I roll my eyes at him, but recognize I'm growing more at ease with Luke's attention.

After caffeine loading, we head out. During the run, I gather my thoughts about what I need to ask him. I estimate we run about three miles before I stop.

"Someone's been practicing." Luke barely pants for air.

"A little," I pant. "I have a question for you."

"Okay."

"You made a comment the other night about not wanting to have kids." I pause to see if he will volunteer additional information.

"Did I? I don't remember."

He's not making this any easier, but I have to ask. "Is that true? Do you not want kids? Do you not want to be a dad?"

"I never thought I'd be a very good father. I'm pretty busy, and it's not like I had a great role model growing up." He bends over to stretch his muscles. "I like being around the kids at the center, but I don't need my own."

"Oh." Luke has always had a difficult relationship with his dad, but I had no idea it had affected him like this. I could tell him I believe he'd be an excellent father, or point out that the joy he experiences working with the kids at the center could be a sign it's something he'd enjoy in his personal life, but I don't. I'm afraid if I say these things, he'll disagree with me.

"Hey." Luke walks over and grabs my chin, forcing me to look in his eyes. "I see the wheels spinning. I like kids, and I really want to meet Amelia. I know I could be a great stepdad.

My not wanting kids of my own is not a reflection on what kind of relationship I could have with her."

I give a half-smile. He's being honest, and he believes this is what I'm worried about, but he's wrong. I have no doubt he would be good with Amelia. He wouldn't be in my life if I thought he wasn't capable of that. But what if, despite everything that's right between the two of us, there's something that hinders us being able to move forward? Having children or not is a big thing not to agree about. Luke has made his feelings clear. I won't say anything prematurely, but I need to figure out exactly what I want.

Chapter 17

When I arrive at my office Monday morning, Ryan is there. He's carrying on a conversation with Linda about yesterday's Chargers game, but I presume he has been waiting to see me.

"Good morning, Linda, Ryan." I walk past them directly into my office.

He follows me in and shuts the door behind him. "I came to apologize. I was out of line the other day."

"Thank you. You don't understand the situation." I turn on my computer and put my purse in a desk drawer.

"Maybe not, but I hope you do."

I sigh and sit down. I fold my hands, placing them on top of my desk. "I've known Luke for a long time. We went to high school together. More than that, he was my boyfriend."

"Seriously?" Ryan's eyes grow wide.

"We ran into each other at our high school reunion, he ended up investing in the winery, and things happened from there." There is a long pause while Ryan processes what I've told him.

"I guess his reaction to me does make a little more sense then."

I nod in understanding. "He has a very bold personality."

"I don't want to make you mad." Ryan hesitates. "I don't know much about Luke, but he seems pretty arrogant and intense."

"I appreciate the concern. Like I said, I've known him a long time. I know what I'm getting myself into."

"Then I'll back off."

"Thank you. I really would like to continue our friendship if you can handle that."

"I'm guessing your new boyfriend won't like that very much."

"You behave yourself, and I'll deal with him."

"What are you going to wear?" Luke sounds frustrated. I can hear him shuffling papers in the background.

"I planned on wearing my lingerie nurse outfit, but don't worry, I'll put a coat over it."

"Are you trying to be funny, or do you want me to jump in my plane and come down there?"

"I'm going to wear jeans, a sweatshirt, and boots. I'm taking my daughter trick-or-treating, not going to the Playboy Mansion."

"Yes, trick-or-treating with your husband."

"Don't say it like that. All the paperwork has been filed. We're only waiting for the final stamp from the judge."

"Right. But let's talk more about this nurse's outfit of yours."

"Sorry, no sexy nurse outfit in my closet."

"Well now I know what I want for Christmas."

"You want a sexy nurse outfit to wear? Wow, that's kinky, even for you." I smile.

"Oh, trust me, you haven't seen anything yet."

I can practically hear his smirk through the phone. "Every time I think I say something shocking or funny, you top me." I pout.

"I like topping you." His husky voice makes heat rise in my face.

"I have to go. Some of us have real work to do and don't get to fly around the world for a living," I tease. He's not happy about me meeting up with Grant and humor is my diversion tactic.

"I'm not traveling this week. San Francisco's only a short flight away. Very easy to come down there if you keep tempting me with all this talk of lingerie." Luke pauses, and I hear voices in the background. "I have to go too. Contrary to your assumptions that I only fly around all the time, I have actual work to do as well. I'll see you this weekend at the groundbreaking ceremony."

"Okay."

"And afterward, you can put on your sexy nurse costume for me."

"No sexy nurse costume."

"We'll see."

After we hang up, I go online to search for a costume.

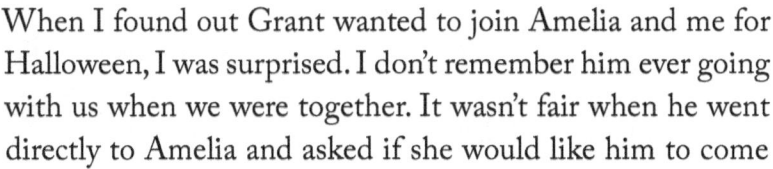

When I found out Grant wanted to join Amelia and me for Halloween, I was surprised. I don't remember him ever going with us when we were together. It wasn't fair when he went directly to Amelia and asked if she would like him to come with us. I couldn't say no when she displayed genuine excitement at the idea.

The doorbell rings as I'm finishing our mini photo session in the family room. When I told Luke I didn't take photographs anymore, that wasn't entirely true; I take a ton of Amelia. When Amelia squeals and runs to the door, I know I've made the right decision letting Grant tag along.

She opens the door and jumps into his not-quite-ready arms.

He struggles to catch her. "There's my Batgirl." He gives her a big hug and then returns her to the floor.

"I am not Batgirl, I'm Batman." She points at the yellow emblem on her black leotard.

He looks at me and raises an eyebrow.

"Apparently, Amelia and I will spend the winter studying all the great feminists," I say with a smile. "I couldn't get her to wear the skirt."

He smiles but doesn't laugh. It never dawned on me until this moment how infrequently he laughs. Maybe he simply doesn't find me particularly funny. I'm trying to remember if he laughs at other people's jokes when Amelia interrupts.

"Let's go, Mom!" she yells, racing off to get her orange plastic bucket.

"Let me grab my keys." I follow her to the kitchen.

"You didn't dress up this year," Grant states matter-of-factly when I return.

My mind flashes to the nurse's costume I ordered a couple of days ago. "My costume this year isn't appropriate for trick-or-treating with kids."

I walk past Grant and out the front door, noticing the redness that has flushed his face.

"How was spending time with Grant last night?" Linda asks as I refill my water bottle. It's only ten in the morning, and I'm already on my third bottle. My increased thirst must be a result of all the sugar I ate.

"It was fine. With Amelia there he couldn't bring up anything too serious." I stop in front of her desk. "Can I ask you something?"

"Of course."

"You've been around Grant several times."

"Yeah?"

"Has he always been so dull?"

She laughs out loud. "Oh dear. Has divorce led you to some revelations about the good doctor?"

"Maybe. He's pleasant enough, but he's not very fun, is he?"

She laughs harder. "No. Fun isn't the word I would use to describe him."

"What word would you use?"

"Responsible?" She can barely get the words out between giggles. "Serious?"

"Sturdy?" I picture all the solid wood furniture Grant selected for our home over the years. He'd assured me they were investment pieces and would last forever. I thought they were clunky and lacked character.

"Oh dear." Linda's laughter fills the room. "Dr. Dull?"

She and I quickly quiet our laughter when Mrs. Bianchi pops into our office.

"Glad you ladies are enjoying your day." She smiles.

"What can we help you with, Mrs. Bianchi?" I still have a wide grin plastered on my face.

"I came by to make sure you're both attending the ground-breaking tomorrow."

"Of course," I say.

"I'll be here too." Linda nods.

"It's my weekend with Amelia, so I'm going to bring her for part of it. Grant will pick her up later in the afternoon to take her to a birthday party."

"Great! I haven't seen Amelia in a while." Mrs. Bianchi has always enjoyed having her around the winery. I assume it reminds her of her own kids running around here many years ago. "I'll see you both tomorrow then." She leaves.

"Grant is coming tomorrow?" Linda sounds surprised, and I hear a little apprehension in her voice.

"Just to pick up Amelia."

"And Luke will be here too?" Linda's eyes widen.

"It's not a big deal." I attempt to dismiss her concern with a wave of my hand. Linda doesn't appear convinced. "Don't look at me like that. It'll be fine."

"I guess we know Grant's tendency toward the uninteresting didn't rub off on you," Linda calls to me as I return to my office.

―――――

Once again, I find myself having to be up early on a Saturday. I jog downstairs to make a cup of tea. Amelia is already in the family room, watching cartoons.

"Morning, love bug." I grab a big mug from the cabinet.

"Morning, Mom." She stays focused on the television. "What are we doing today?"

"We're going to the winery for a while, and then Dad is going to pick you up and take you to Sam's birthday party." I pour milk into the steamer. "You need to make her a card to go with her gift."

"I will," Amelia answers, again without looking at me.

"Amelia, we still have lots to do before we leave today. Please go get the stuff to make her card." She's still glued to the colorful action on the screen. I raise my voice to get her attention. "Amelia Jane."

"Sorry, mom." She turns off the screen and marches up the stairs.

We arrive at the winery while final preparations for the groundbreaking are taking place. Luke sounded excited on the phone last night when I mentioned I was bringing Amelia today, but then I ruined it by telling him I wasn't ready to introduce him as my boyfriend yet. Not today, not in front of everyone. His mood soured even more when I told him Grant would be stopping by.

Luke and Aaron are already here and appear to be discussing business, based on the serious expressions they wear. Linda is standing with Andre, our events coordinator. I greet her first, and Andre rushes away to handle some crisis.

"How's my favorite eight-year-old?" Linda says when she sees Amelia.

"Linda!" Amelia screams as she runs to give her a big hug.

"How's my favorite boss this morning? Ready for all the excitement?" Linda peers at me over Amelia.

"I'm good. It's exciting to officially kickoff construction." I glance at the other side of the lawn where Luke is.

"That's not the excitement I'm referring to," Linda says.

"I'm going to a mini golf birthday party for my best friend, Sam, today," Amelia chimes in. "She's turning eight, and I bought her the coolest gift ever."

"Did you get her a pony?" Linda asks wearing a serious expression.

"No." Amelia laughs brightly. "I got her nail polishes and a nail dryer and those weird things that go between your toes so they don't get messed up."

"Did you get me some nail polish too?" Linda teases Amelia.

"No." Amelia looks embarrassed until she catches on. "It's not your birthday, Linda."

"It's not, but I like nail polish."

"I'll bring you some next time. Mom, can we buy Linda some nail polish?"

"Sure. I bet Linda would like the dark blue you picked out for Sam. We'll get her one of those."

Linda scrunches up her face. "Dark blue? Doesn't that make it look like your fingertips are frozen?"

"Oh, Linda." Amelia shakes her head.

"Linda, can you take Amelia to get something to drink from the restaurant while I have a word with Mrs. Bianchi?" I hope she will catch on to my real reason for distracting Amelia for a few minutes.

"Of course, but only if I can get her a cookie too."

Amelia peers up at me, fidgeting with excitement as she awaits my answer.

"Sure," I say reluctantly. I always intend to reduce the amount of sugar Amelia eats, and it never seems to go according to plan.

After they leave, I join Luke and Aaron. "Hi, beautiful," he says when I'm still several feet away.

I smile and tuck my hair behind my ear. "Good morning."

"Good morning, Jessica." Aaron gives me a half-smile before returning his attention to Luke. "We need to fix this before it becomes a bigger problem."

"I know. I'll go out there this week and get everything straightened out."

"And if you can't?" This is the most serious I've ever seen Aaron.

"Then we talk to our lawyers and find a way out." Frustration radiates from Luke.

"That's not a road I'd like to go down," Aaron says.

Luke sighs. "Me neither. I'll try to avoid getting the lawyers involved. No sense worrying about it until I meet with them and see how serious they are."

"I don't think I need to spell out what this would do to the company."

"No, I know what's at stake, and I told you I'll take care of it."

"Fine. We can talk more about this later." Aaron takes a deep breath. "Sorry, Jessica. How are you this morning?"

"I'm doing well," I answer.

"Great. I'll let you two have a minute." Aaron leaves us.

Luke is rubbing the back of his neck.

"What was that about?" I ask.

Luke cracks his neck. "One of our other investments. They found a loophole in our contract with them and are trying to screw us over. I need to go have a face-to-face with them. See if we can come up with a reasonable compromise."

"I've never seen Aaron like that."

"We dumped a large portion of our reserves into this venture. If we get no return on it, the company will be in serious trouble."

I start to reach out to touch him, but I remember Amelia will be back any minute and retract my hand.

Luke frowns at me. "Perfect. To top off my shitty morning, I have to pretend we're simply colleagues. This is…never mind. We can't discuss this here."

I can tell he's avoiding eye contact with me. "Are you mad? I thought you understood my position on waiting to tell Amelia." I cross my arms defensively.

"Not mad…frustrated."

"I don't know how to make this better for you right now," I say stiffly.

"I don't suppose you can sneak away for a few hours this evening?" Luke gives me a hopeful glance.

"I have Amelia tonight," I remind him.

"Right."

I start to say that maybe I can talk my mom into taking Amelia out to dinner to give us some time, but Linda and Amelia are quickly approaching. Amelia has chocolate in the corners of her mouth.

"Looks like someone had a chocolate chip cookie." I smile at my messy girl.

"Good guess, Mom. Actually, I had two."

"That was supposed to be our secret." Linda pretends to whisper in Amelia's ear but says it loud enough for Luke and me to hear.

"Oops." Amelia uses her sweetest voice.

I can't help but laugh, and I'm surprised when Luke joins in.

"You two are trouble." I put my hands on my hips and pretend to be mad. Amelia knows I'm kidding and giggles. "Amelia, I'd like you to meet Luke."

"Hi, Luke." She smiles at him and sticks out a hand.

"Nice to meet you, Amelia." He shakes her hand.

"Do you work here?"

"Kind of, but not really. It's sort of complicated."

She nods like she understands completely. "A lot of things with adults are complicated, aren't they?"

"Sometimes."

"My parents use that word a lot."

"Amelia, Luke and I went to high school together." I want her to know more about him, but I'm not ready to tell her everything yet.

"Cool. Were you friends?"

"We were." Luke smiles.

"But then you weren't?" Amelia frowns.

"And then we weren't." Luke matches her frown.

"What happened? Was Mom mean to you?"

"No."

"Then were you mean to her?"

"Unfortunately, I was."

Amelia considers his answer for a minute. "Did you say you were sorry?"

"Yes, but not for a long time."

"But you *did*, right?"

"Yes."

"Now you can be friends again. Mom always says we have to forgive people when they apologize." She gazes up at me, and my heart clenches.

"Yes, we're friends again." Luke smiles again, and she smiles back.

"Welcome to Bianchi Winery everyone!" Mrs. Bianchi's voice booms from the speakers.

"Let's go find a seat. The ceremony is about to start." Luke offers his hand to Amelia, who freely places it in his.

After Mrs. Bianchi gives her speech and tosses the first shovel of dirt on the specially laid blanket, music from the band fills the air, and the guests mingle on the lawn. Amelia runs off to join a game of tag with other kids in attendance. I recognize many of the attendees from previous meetings and functions, including the young woman who was trying so hard to maintain Luke's attention the night of the investor dinner. She doesn't approach Luke though. She appears to be keeping an eye on Ryan instead.

I'm asking Aaron how Andi is when Luke joins us and hands me a glass of red wine. I don't bother to ask which kind, because I like all the reds Bianchi Winery produces.

"We will have to plan a double date next time you're in San Francisco," Aaron says right before Amelia appears.

"That would be great." I motion to her to wait a minute. She fidgets impatiently.

"Mom," Amelia interrupts, even though I haven't given her my attention yet.

"What Amelia?"

"Dad's here."

I signal an apology to the others and leave to meet Grant. I'm too much of a coward to watch Luke's reaction.

Amelia and I cross the lawn to where Grant is waiting for us.

"Thank you again for taking her," I say.

"No problem. Ready?" He pulls her into a hug. She laughs and wriggles until he releases her.

We walk toward my car in silence. When we're close enough, I unlock the door and Amelia gets her stuff.

"You brought Luke today." Grant tries to sound casual, but I'm sure I hear irritation in his voice.

"Not exactly. He's an investor at the winery. I haven't told Amelia anything about us yet, so please don't say anything."

"That's interesting."

"Why is that interesting? I think her parents getting divorced is painful enough without bringing other people into the mix."

Grant flinches. "Are you mad I introduced her to Stephanie?"

"Would it matter if I was? Thinking of my feelings certainly hasn't been a priority of yours."

He starts to respond but drops the subject when Amelia returns, carrying her gift for the party. "Let's go, kid."

Amelia gives me a hug. I release her and am surprised when Grant embraces me. I haven't had any physical contact with him in months. It feels familiar but not necessarily comfortable. Like wearing a pair of old jeans that are now too small. The hug goes on a couple of seconds too long. I want to pull away, but I'm aware Amelia is watching us.

"Yes, well, thank you again, Grant. I really appreciate it." I force my voice into an unnaturally high pitch, trying to sound nonchalant.

He finally releases me and walks Amelia to his car.

I return to the party. I can tell from the stiffness in his stance that Luke saw the whole thing. His hands are in his pockets, preventing me from taking one. His expression is hard. He keeps his attention on Aaron.

"Luke." I place a hand on his arm. He doesn't react.

"I'm going to give you two a minute." Aaron shoots Luke a look of warning before strolling away.

Luke sighs. "I understand the Amelia situation—I do. She is pretty amazing, by the way." His expression softens for a moment.

It warms my insides, remembering their earlier interaction.

"But Grant is another issue. I don't want to witness you being overly affectionate with your ex." He stares at me unflinchingly.

"Overly affectionate? That's an exaggeration." I place my hands on my hips.

"I don't see you hugging Aaron or Mr. Bianchi like that, and I better not see you hug Ryan like that. Speaking of which, I'm quickly losing patience with your 'friend' and his inability to keep his eyes off what's mine." Luke is tightly focused on me. He's taken his hands out of his pockets, and I can see they are clenched.

"Back up. Grant hugged me. I wasn't expecting it, but it was only a goodbye hug."

"So I guess if another woman hugged me goodbye like that, you wouldn't have a problem with it?"

"It was a simple hug."

"If you say so." He shrugs.

"As for Ryan, I'll have another talk with him."

"No, I'll have a talk with him this time." His tone is icy.

"I know you're frustrated, but remember this is a work function."

"Right." Luke downs the rest of the wine from his glass. "I don't want to fight with you. Let's talk about this later."

"Fine," I agree. "I need to run to the restroom. I'll meet you back here."

My trip to the restroom takes longer than anticipated when I run into Mrs. Everett. We spend several minutes chatting before she excuses herself to find Mrs. Bianchi. When I return to the party, I scan the crowd to find Luke. He has his back to me as I join the group of people he's with.

"Definitely glad I don't have to deal with that," Luke shakes his head, and the group laughs.

"What's happening?" I ask, feeling left out.

"We were watching that family over there. The little boy threw a major tantrum because his dad told him he couldn't have a glass of the 'special grape juice' everyone else is drinking," Monica says.

"I asked if anyone thought the parents were regretting their decision not to enjoy a day alone," Ryan adds.

"Oh," is all I manage to say.

"That kid did put on quite a display." Aaron attempts to defend Luke's comment.

I glare at Luke. His eyes are glassy, and I can tell he's had too much to drink. He continues to talk to Monica about the "awful" child, oblivious to the fact that his comments are not being well received by me. Ryan, on the other hand, appears positively thrilled that Luke is displaying such an unflattering side of himself. I can't decide who I'm more disappointed in, Luke or Ryan. Suddenly, I don't have much of an interest in making small talk with any of these people.

Linda joins the gathering and I'm grateful to have someone to talk to. I ask about her plans for the rest of the weekend. I'm genuinely interested, but it also distracts from the others. At some point, Luke must realize he's had enough wine, because he switches to water. I don't talk to him the rest of the afternoon.

"I have to pick up Amelia," I say after my phone finally chimes and gives me an excuse to escape.

"I'll walk you to your car," Luke quickly offers.

I say goodbye to Linda, Monica, and Aaron. I purposely don't say anything to Ryan.

I'm pressing the unlock button on my key fob when Luke finally breaks the silence.

"Come here." He pulls me into his chest. Tears fill my eyes, but I manage to control them. "I acted like an ass earlier. I know this situation is difficult for you too."

I don't say anything, but I continue to let him hold me.

"It's hard for me to be around you and not show my feelings for you. It's difficult for me to watch Ryan and Grant react to you and not be able to say anything."

"You can't be jealous of every guy who looks at me." I don't remove my face from his chest.

"I'm not. I overreacted about Ryan, and I'll figure out the Grant situation. I know he has to be around, and I'll learn to deal with it better."

I pull away, but he maintains a grip on my arms. His eyes thoroughly search mine.

"We had an off day. It happens." It's unclear who he's trying to convince. "I messed today up. I'm sorry. Do you want me to come over tonight?"

"I have Amelia." I'm sad, not because he can't come over, but because I don't want him to. I need some space to think.

"I know...I just thought..." He sighs and stares at his feet. "I have to travel this week, but I can come back next weekend. We can talk and figure stuff out."

"Okay."

He kisses me on the forehead.

"I have to go," I say as his lips break contact.

"I know." The unmistakable sadness in his voice is painful.

Chapter 18

The remainder of the weekend is spent in mom mode. I help Amelia finish her book report on *Charlotte's Web* and clean the house. It gives me the opportunity to think about Luke. We still have issues. Issues, I worry, we may not be able to overcome. I can't be the girlfriend he wants right now. I'm not sure he can be the husband I will want later. One thing I learned from my divorce is the importance of each individual getting what they need out of a relationship. I may want another child someday. If I'm not honest about that now, it will cause problems and heartache later.

I don't feel any better after my marathon cleaning session, so I go for a run. I have no choice but to bring Amelia with me. She won't make it far, but a short run may be better than nothing. She is enthusiastic for exactly one block. After that she is too tired to continue. We return home, her with complaints of sore legs and me without any sense of clarity.

Luke is traveling to Texas this week, which supplies me with a good excuse to put off the conversation I'm not looking forward to having. We text and call throughout the week but keep the conversations light. He mentions he misses me several times. I miss him too. I begin to hope that maybe this weekend he'll change his mind about having kids. Before I get too eager, I remind myself he's made it clear he doesn't want children. I need to stop ignoring what I simply don't want to hear.

It's Thursday before Linda calls me out on my distractedness.

"What's going on with you? Did Luke do something?" She closes my office door behind her.

"Luke's fine. It's me." I sigh and slouch in my chair. "I don't know if we want the same things."

"Like what?"

"You know, life…kids. We live in different cities and have totally different lifestyles."

"I'm sure a change in location is not a deal-breaker for him, especially considering how much he travels. Does he not want kids?"

"No." She frowns, so I quickly clarify. "He says he pictures himself as a stepdad but doesn't want any of his own."

"Oh. Well, do you want more kids?"

"I don't know. Maybe."

"And what did he say?"

"I haven't told him yet."

"So you're this worked up without even talking to him about it?"

"He's been very clear about not wanting kids." I sit up.

"We all say lots of things we end up changing our minds about. You won't know until you actually talk to him about it."

"I'm afraid," I admit. I grab a paperclip and twist it into an unrecognizable shape.

"Of what?"

"That he will say something I don't want to hear. Something that will make it clear I have to walk away." I keep my eyes trained on my abstract art.

"Because you don't want to."

"I don't want to, but I also don't want to be in another doomed relationship." I set the paperclip down.

"For what it's worth, I don't think your relationship with Luke is doomed. I've often found that things like this work themselves out in unexpected ways."

"But sometimes they don't. Sometimes people end up heartbroken. I worry about going through that again."

"Talk to him. Once you tell him what you're worrying about, he may surprise you. And if he doesn't, then you can move on, knowing you have all the information."

"I plan on talking to him this weekend. He has a meeting Friday night, so I won't see him until Saturday."

"Everything works out how it's supposed to."

"I know, but I'm worried I'm not mentally prepared for what's supposed to be."

She returns to her desk, and I attempt to get some work done. I haven't been the most productive at work this week, so unless I want to take reports home with me, I need to force myself to focus. I'm in the middle of running a revised set of financial statements for October when my cell rings.

It's Grant. The hug at the groundbreaking ceremony was awkward, but overall I believe our relationship is moving toward a successful co-parenting situation.

"Grant." Reports spit out of my printer.

"Hi Jessica. My mom asked if it's okay for Amelia to spend the night at her house tomorrow—"

"Of course. It's your weekend. You don't have to get my approval for Amelia to spend time with her grandparents," I snap.

"Bad day?"

"Sorry."

"It's okay." He pauses. I tap a pencil on my desk, waiting for him to continue. "What I wanted to know is…I thought it might be a good opportunity for us to get together. Tomorrow night, while Amelia is with my parents." He takes a deep breath before finishing. "Will you meet me for dinner?"

"I was about to make plans." I cringe. It's only a half-lie. I was considering calling Vivien and Emily to see if either of them are free.

"So that means you don't have plans yet?" he presses.

"I guess not."

"Great. We need to talk. It's important."

My mind instantly jumps to our daughter. "Does it have to do with Amelia?"

"Yes."

"What's wrong?" My heart races at the mere thought of getting bad news about her.

"Not like that. Nothing's wrong with Amelia. I just want to discuss some things with you."

My heart beats normally again. If the ineptitude of this phone call is any indication of how tomorrow's dinner is going to go, I'm sure I'll be home early. "All right, I can meet you tomorrow after work."

"Let's meet at Palumbo's at six."

"Sounds good. Thanks for asking where I want to go." I mumble the last part.

"What?" Grant either didn't hear what I said or is pretending he didn't.

"Nothing. I'll see you tomorrow night."

I call Luke during the drive home from work. I know he won't be happy about it, but I need to tell him about my dinner with Grant. He answers his phone after only one ring. "You still at the office?"

"For another hour or so. We have one more interview to conduct, then Aaron and I are going to play racquetball."

"Interview?"

"After the debacle in Texas, Aaron and I are considering bringing in another partner. Another set of eyes to review contracts and handle the workload." Luke's meeting with their troubled investment was a mild success. He was able to work out a deal that, while not yielding the financial gain they hoped for, was fair and would keep them out of litigation.

"That's exciting."

"It is."

"I'm afraid what I'm about to say isn't going to put you in a very good mood."

"Okay," he says warily.

"I'm meeting Grant for dinner tomorrow night." I spit the words out quickly, hoping that will somehow soften their impact.

"Was this family dinner his idea?"

"Not a family dinner. Just the two of us." I take a calming breath. "He wants to talk."

He doesn't say anything for what seems like a long time. It has probably only been several seconds, but his silence is more unbearable than anything he could say to me right now.

"Luke?"

"I'm not sure what you expect me to say." I picture him running his hand through his hair.

"We have a child together. He does have to be a part of my life to some degree."

"I don't see you two meeting for dinner as necessary."

"It's not like I'm excited about it. He said he needs to discuss some important business. It's probably about the house." I listen to him breathe for a few seconds. We both know a discussion about the house wouldn't require meeting in person.

"Honestly, you're putting me in a bad position. I'm either the jealous asshole boyfriend who is making this situation harder, or I'm the idiot who says I'm fine with you having dinner with your ex."

"I can't win either way. I feel bad no matter what I do." I can't think of anything to say to make either of us feel better about it, so I change the subject. "Are you still coming over this weekend?"

"I have that meeting in Irvine tomorrow night. I was planning on coming to your house Saturday."

"Sounds good."

"Can you do me one favor?"

"Maybe?" I attempt to sound playful, hoping he is about to make one of the comments that make me blush.

"Don't wear anything blue."

"Why?"

"You look amazing in blue. Don't waste it on him."

"No blue," I agree. "I'll stick to black."

"That doesn't really help. You look great in black too."

"Would you like to pick out my outfit then?" I offer one last-ditch attempt to bring out his naughty side.

"You're capable of choosing."

"I'll call you tomorrow night, after I get home." I don't know what else I can say to ease his discomfort.

I arrive for dinner ten minutes early and am surprised to see Grant has beaten me here. When we were together, he always seemed to get stuck with a patient or something else more important. There were many nights I sat and waited in restaurants for him. I figured tonight would be a reminder of those times.

He sees me, smiles, and stands. He looks like he can't decide whether he should give me a hug or not. Thankfully, he doesn't. We slide into the booth. I pretend to check my phone for missed calls or texts. I look around the crowded restaurant—everywhere except at the man I should know better than anyone. He feels like a stranger.

I can't watch the room all night, so I brave a view of the table. Grant has already ordered a bottle of Chianti. Not my favorite, but I would drink a glass of almost anything right now to take the edge off.

We busy ourselves reading the menu even though we always get the same thing here. The waiter appears. We both order the jalapeno cream chicken.

"This place looks the same as it did when we first started coming here." Grant takes a sip of wine.

"Yep. Some places stand the test of time," I agree.

"Some relationships do too." He peers over the top of his glass at me.

My eyes grow wide, and I can practically taste the bile rising in my throat. "Grant, get it over with so I can pretend to be happy for you and go home."

"What? Oh no, I'm not talking about Stephanie and me." He drinks more wine. "I was talking about us."

"I don't think that's an appropriate sentiment for a divorced couple." I press my lips tightly together.

"Not divorced yet," he reminds me.

"Where are you going with this?" I place my folded hands on the table. I'm already tired of whatever game we're playing.

"Hear me out." He always starts this way when he's about to say something I won't like or agree with. "I've been thinking a lot about you the last several weeks."

"I'm not sure Stephanie would love to hear that." I'm instantly embarrassed it sounds like I care.

"We ended things a couple weeks ago." He waves, as if to dismiss their relationship as inconsequential.

I wonder if he waves like that when he talks about our marriage. "Oh." I would say I'm sorry, but I'm not.

"I didn't come to talk about her. I would like to talk about us." He clears his throat. "We never talked much about our breakup."

"Once you admitted to the affair, there wasn't a lot left to say." I fidget with the clasp on my bracelet.

"I thought we would at least talk. I was shocked when you left and didn't even ask why I did it."

"I have no interest in hearing what another woman gave you that I couldn't." I glare at him, and he flinches.

"I wasn't a very good husband to you." He rubs his hands together.

I keep a scowl on my face so he knows he's going to need to say something more than that. I did not come here for this, but since I'm here, I might as well let the man say what he wants to say.

He refills our wine glasses. "Over the years, we started living separate lives. You were focused on work and Amelia. In hindsight, I see how wrapped up I was in my practice. I blamed you. I thought you were the one who changed. I saw myself as the one who had provided you a good life with the family you always wanted. I became angry that it somehow wasn't enough."

His words are unexpected. We haven't had an open and honest conversation about our relationship in a very long time. It's easier to be honest when you don't have anything to lose.

I give a small smile, remembering the beginning of our marriage. "I was so happy when we first got married and had Amelia. We were both busy with school and work and trying to figure out how to take care of this little human they let us take home, even though we had no idea what we were doing. It was crazy and chaotic, but I was happy."

"I was happy too." He gives me a sad smile.

"Then you finished school. You began working long hours to build your practice. I missed you, and things were different, but I couldn't complain about it. You were doing something important. I decided to fade into the background for a while until you got established in your new career. Unfortunately, what I saw as a temporary arrangement became our new normal."

"I didn't know you felt that way. I wish you would have said something. I thought you were disinterested in my career and later, in me." There is a long pause while he drains his glass again. "Eventually, I sought out people who were interested in me and what I was doing. First colleagues, and then later, well, you know."

"Maybe if I would've said something, you wouldn't have…" I wipe a few tears away.

"I should have said something. I didn't realize how bad we were at communicating until after you left and I was forced to examine what happened." He wipes moisture from the corner of his eye. "Jess, I know it's not a good reason, but I wanted to feel like I was making someone happy again. I made a big mistake, and I'm truly sorry."

My breath catches, and for a moment I can't breathe.

"That's the first time you've said you were sorry about it." My words come out in a whisper. I didn't realize until this moment how badly I needed to hear those words from him.

"I've said sorry."

"No you haven't." I stare down at the table.

"Then I'm sorry for that too." He has the most anguished expression I have ever seen him wear. My chest squeezes and the pain prompts me to look away.

There are no more words after the avalanche of regrets that has buried us. Our stillness contrasts with the bustle of the restaurant. A table of teenagers laughs. A waiter hurries to drop off plates of pasta before they get cold. A mother attempts to bribe her toddler to eat "one more bite" of his now soggy dinner so he can have ice cream for dessert. Our grief doesn't belong in this space.

"Jess, I want to try to make it right."

"What does that mean?"

"I want Amelia to grow up with both her parents."

He knows how I feel about my father not being around. I'm irritated he's attempting to use it to his advantage.

"She does have both her parents. I haven't killed you yet." I attempt to lighten the mood with a little divorce humor.

"I mean in the same house."

I roll my eyes at him.

"What?" Grant looks confused.

"You never laugh at anything I say," I complain.

"I don't find you joking about killing me particularly funny," he states plainly. "Don't you want Amelia to grow up with the family you didn't have?"

"Low blow, Grant."

"I didn't mean it to be. I just assumed you would want that for Amelia. Especially considering how much being from a broken home has affected you."

"What's that supposed to mean?"

"Never mind. We don't need to get into that tonight."

"Actually, I think we do now." It's suddenly too warm, so I take off my black cardigan.

Grant pinches his lips together. "I didn't come here tonight to put you on the defensive."

"I'm not defensive." I spit the words at him and toss my sweater next to me. "I cannot wait to hear your explanation of my daddy issues."

"Your dad leaving affected you more than you like to admit, that's all."

"I disagree. My father gets no credit for how I turned out, good or bad." I stare at him, unblinking.

"I will undoubtedly regret this, but name one man in your life you trust." Grant leans forward on his folded arms.

"I have plenty of men in my life I trust."

Grant stares me down. "Name one."

"I trusted you." I stare back, chin lifted.

"Not completely." He leans back, shaking his head.

"Yes, I did."

"Why didn't you tell me about your secret savings account?"

During the course of our divorce, Grant found out about a savings account I set up when we were first married. I would stash away small amounts of money periodically along with any unexpected bonuses I received at the winery.

"I told you already. I set up that account and planned on surprising you with it when we retired."

"Bullshit. It was your backup plan. Your escape strategy, in case I let you down."

"And you did." My voice rises, and I remind myself we're in a public place.

"That's not the point."

"It's not?"

"Truth is, you always have it in the back of your mind that people, primarily men, are going to let you down. You assume if you're prepared for it, you'll be able to stop it—or at least it won't hurt as bad."

"I trust Mr. Bianchi." I reach for my glass of water.

"Yes, but you trust him because you trust Mrs. Bianchi. I honestly don't think you would have taken the job had he been the one running the winery."

"So because I found a great job, and I happen to be working for a strong woman, it must mean I have issues working for men? That's ridiculous." I drink ice water, trying to cool myself down. "I'm friends with Ryan."

"Ryan is one you should be suspicious of. That guy has ulterior motives, but that's not the point. It's not that you don't get along with men, it's that you don't trust them."

"Let's say it's all true. What's wrong with being prepared?"

He finally laughs, except I haven't said anything funny. "Nothing. Being worried all the time that every man is going to leave you doesn't leave a lot of room for a happy relationship. Aren't you exhausted?"

"I *am* exhausted. I'm tired of being here."

"We were married for eight years, and you never got to a place where you really opened up to me."

"Yes, I did. I shared all my work successes with you. I loved sharing in all of Amelia's accomplishments with you."

"Exactly. You shared the good things. Never anything bad or scary or painful."

"Well shit, I'm sorry for not adding more drama to your life." A sardonic laugh escapes me.

"It's not drama. It's letting other people support you. I suppose that's it, isn't it? You assume if things get too difficult, any man is going to bail."

"Like you?" I lower my head so he can't see the fresh tears accumulating in my eyes. I hear a deep inhalation from across the table, followed by a controlled release of breath.

"Sometimes men leave, but sometimes they realize they made the biggest mistake of their life." He reaches across the table and grabs my clenched hands. "I can't take back what I did, but I am very sorry."

I don't want to look at him, so I allow the tears to fall on my blouse.

"Don't cry." He softens his tone. "I didn't realize what our problems were at the time, so I dealt with them in the worst way possible. Without meaning to, I confirmed your worst fears." He squeezes my hands, and I look up. "I want a chance to make it right. I want to earn your trust back. I know I can do better, and we can be the happy family you always wanted. The family you and Amelia deserve."

I let him hold my hands as more tears spill down my cheeks. I haven't seen this sincere, affectionate side of Grant in a very long time. I thought this side of him was gone, that it died as he aged. This is the Grant I fell in love with.

Chapter 19

My head is pounding. I squint against the sunlight streaming through my bedroom window—the window I forgot to close last night. That explains why my room is like an icebox and I've created a cocoon out of my blankets.

Knock! Knock! Knock!

I'm startled by the intense beating my front door is taking. It's a physical manifestation of my troubled head. I should not have drunk more wine when I got home last night. I should not have taken the ibuprofen containing a sleep aid either. The sloppy combination has left me feeling like a zombie.

Knock! Knock! Knock!

"Hold on!" I yell, though I have no idea if the person attempting to break down my door can hear me.

I clumsily unwind myself from my blankets and throw on my robe. I take a quick glance at myself in the bathroom mirror. My appearance reflects the sick sensation swirling in my stomach.

Knock! Knock! Knock!

"I'm coming," I announce, carefully making my way down the stairs. I don't remember them being so steep. I reach the door as the assailant pummels it again.

"Seriously, what…?" I freeze.

Luke is standing on the doorstep with hands clenched into fists and narrowed eyes. I passed out without calling him last night, and by the looks of things, he doesn't appreciate my cowardice.

"I would like to say I'm surprised by your lack of enthusiasm to see me." He squeezes his eyes shut. "Be honest. Are you alone?"

"I told you Amelia was spending the weekend—oh, you're not asking about Amelia, are you?"

"No."

"I don't like what you're insinuating." I place my hands on my hips.

"And I don't like that my girlfriend had dinner with her ex-husband, didn't bother to call me afterward, and now won't let me in her house for some unknown reason." His eyes are an icy shade of blue.

"I'm sorry, come in. I'm hung over, so I'm not quite up to speed with your anger yet." I step aside.

"Must have been a super fun night," he mutters as he passes me.

"I should have called you. It was a very overwhelming night, and I came home, by myself, and drank too much." I follow him to the family room.

"You telling me the night was overwhelming doesn't sit much better than saying it was fun."

"Do you want honesty or should I only say what you want to hear?" I blurt. I take a deep breath. "That wasn't fair."

Luke sits on the sofa, and I choose the chair across from him.

I take a deep breath, begging for it to go directly to my brain and stop the throbbing. "Dinner with Grant wasn't what I expected."

"How so?"

"We haven't talked much about our divorce. I didn't plan on that being the goal last night, but it was the outcome. Things got... emotional. Grant told me things he hadn't before. He apologized."

"He never said he was sorry until last night? The guy cheats and doesn't even offer an apology? He sounds amazing," Luke mocks.

"Yeah, well, he didn't. I never gave him much opportunity to. I was so hurt, I just left. Thinking back, he may have tried, but I changed the subject every time." My intention is not to defend Grant, but I know that's what it sounds like.

Luke pinches the bridge of his nose and closes his eyes. "So he finally apologized. Did it make you feel better?"

"Yes...no...I don't know."

I tell him most of my conversation with Grant, leaving out the part about him wanting a second chance. When I'm done we sit in silence, letting our minds work without daring to say our thoughts out loud.

At last he says, "I suppose you would call me a hypocrite if I said he shouldn't be searching for validation elsewhere. However, I will point out that I was eighteen years old when I was seeking that attention. He's a grown man. A man with a family, who should have his shit together by now."

"Yes, he should." I wasn't comparing the two events and am surprised Luke is.

"You could say I was looking for attention all these years. What I did as a single man is in no way comparable to his behavior."

"You're right, it's not."

"Sounds like he's justifying his behavior because you didn't feed his fragile ego." Luke crosses his muscular arms.

"I don't think he was trying to justify it. He was only trying to explain his side." As soon as I say the words, I regret them.

His face tightens. "Why are you defending him?"

"I'm not. I'm simply trying to absorb everything."

"So after all his cheating confessions, you decided to come home, get drunk, and not call me?"

"I planned to call you after I settled down. There was more that happened at dinner."

"That was my guess." His words are clipped and angry.

My heart races. "There is no easy way to say this, so I'm just going to blurt it out. He wants a second chance."

Luke doesn't appear surprised. "That much I could have guessed by the way he hugged you goodbye at the ground-breaking. When he invited you to dinner, I figured he was going to enter his plea. What I can't wrap my head around is why you didn't call me. The only explanation I can come up with is you're considering going back to him." Luke closes his eyes. "Please tell me I'm wrong."

"It's really complicated."

"Is it?" He leans forward and makes sure I'm focusing on him before he continues. "I love you, and I know you love me too."

I'm startled by his admission. He hasn't said those words directly to me in over ten years.

"I have to consider—"

"You can't be serious." He drops his head into his hands.

"Luke...he's Amelia's father."

"Yes, and the way a divorce works is he would still be her father, whether you're with him or not."

"Of course." I clasp my hands together in an effort to still them. "I grew up in a divorced family, and it was awful."

"You grew up with a father who was selfish and absent. I'm not a huge fan of Grant's, but as far as I can tell, he's a good dad. He'll be that whether you're married to him or not. He has proven himself not to be a good husband."

I shake my head in defiance. "You don't understand. This isn't about me. I need to consider what's best for Amelia."

"That's ridiculous. Of course it has to do with you. You can't live your life for someone else, not even Amelia."

"It's not that simple. Being a parent sometimes means making hard decisions. You don't have kids, so maybe you don't understand."

"You're right, I don't understand. I don't know how staying in an unhappy marriage is beneficial for you or your daughter."

"This is why I didn't call you. I can't think clearly around you sometimes." I gaze at the pattern on the area rug. If I look at him, I'll cry, and tears won't help me right now.

"Don't do this. I didn't say it years ago at that party when I should have, but I'm going to say it now. Look at me."

I gaze into Luke's damp eyes. They are filled with pain but also hope. He walks over to me and kneels down so we're face to face.

He holds my hands in his and rubs his thumbs back and forth. "Choose me. I promise to love you more than he ever could. I promise I will make sure you are happy and fulfilled. I promise to work every day to give you the life you deserve. Choose me, Jessica."

Tears stream down my face, and I can't find my voice. He would try, and he would succeed in many ways. My daughter would love him too. Unfortunately, a broken home will have consequences for Amelia, contrary to Luke's opinion. He would do almost anything to make me happy, including sacrificing his own happiness and plans. I can't have him change his life goals and dreams for me. He'll resent me for it someday.

My thoughts paralyze me and my inability to answer breaks him. He lowers his head. He rises but doesn't look at me. He starts to walk away. I miss him already, and he's still in the same room.

"Luke," I whimper. I don't want him to go, but at this point it's not fair to ask him to stay.

He stops but doesn't turn around.

"I hope he knows how lucky he is."

He continues his long walk out of my house. I hear every footstep, like a countdown. The sound of the door shutting behind him is like a gun going off. A gun pointed directly at me. My insides clench, and my lungs struggle to take in enough oxygen. The pressure builds inside me until it has to be released. Since I have no actual bullet hole for the pain to escape through, it escapes through my mouth. I try to catch my breath between the choking sobs.

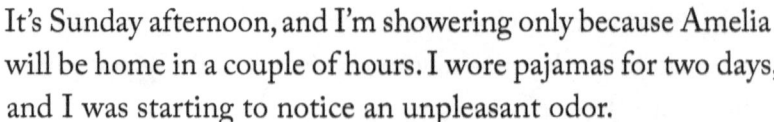

It's Sunday afternoon, and I'm showering only because Amelia will be home in a couple of hours. I wore pajamas for two days, and I was starting to notice an unpleasant odor.

I had a bowl of cereal Saturday night and a banana this morning. My stomach threatened both times to reject the food, but I was able to keep it down. After my shower, I throw a load of laundry in the machine so Amelia has enough clean clothes for the week. I have no interest in doing additional housework. I make a mental note to hire a housekeeper. I have a feeling I'm going to feel like this for a long time.

I consider calling Luke, but I don't have anything to say yet. My continued uncertainty would end up hurting him more. My stomach drops whenever I picture the look on his face when I didn't choose him. When I couldn't choose him. Ironically, I can't bring myself to choose Grant either.

I need to call my mom. My conversations with her usually help.

"What's wrong?" She immediately senses my misery.

"Nothing's wrong. Just wanted to say hi and see how you're doing." I fail in my attempt to sound normal.

"I'm fine. You're obviously not though. What's going on?"

I tell her about my dinner with Grant and my breakup with Luke. She doesn't say anything expect for some "uh-huhs" and "mms."

"I know I made the best decision for Amelia. I guess I just need confirmation," I finish and let out a defeated sigh.

"Honey, it's your decision, but—"

"But what?" She's a great listener, but she doesn't readily offer a lot of advice. When she does, I'm all ears.

"Your decision was based on what you think is best for Amelia?"

"Of course. That's what mothers do."

"Yes, that's often true." She pauses before continuing. "Do you believe Grant is the best decision for you?"

"I don't know." My eyes water again.

"Why do you think your father and I divorced?"

Her question is unexpected. We don't discuss him often, and I've never asked for details about their divorce. He is a lousy father, so I assumed he was an equally lousy husband. "I don't know. He left."

"That's correct, but there's a little more to it than that. He was always arrogant, always thought he knew best. After you were born, he insisted I stay home. Good mothers did that. I only had one more year of college to go before I got my nursing degree, but he was adamant I needed to focus on you. So I stayed home until you started kindergarten. I don't regret those first years I spent with you, going to play-dates and the park, but once you started school, I wanted to go back. So I did. I didn't tell your dad. I knew he wouldn't approve. I found friends to help and took out my own student loans to pay for it. I waited until I graduated to tell him. He was furious. He considered it a betrayal, and I suppose it was. We tried to make it work for a while, but he couldn't get past it...so he left. I wasn't shocked. I knew that was a real possibility when I made my choice, but I did it anyway. I worried about how it could affect you, but I worried about me too and how living a life that wasn't meant for me would affect both of us."

"You never told me any of this. Is this why you were so insistent I finish school after I got pregnant?"

"Yes, but not for me. I knew college was important to you, and I wanted you to finish if you wanted to."

"I never knew why he left."

"You were too young to understand. As you got older, and he stopped making an effort with you, I kept hoping he would realize what he was missing out on. I didn't want to add any fuel to the fire in regard to your strained relationship, so I didn't talk about him a lot. I'm sorry you didn't have the relationship with him you wanted, that you should have had. I blamed myself for a long time."

"It's not your fault he's a crummy father."

"You're right, it's not. Just like it's not your fault Grant cheated on you. It's also not your fault if you realized, through his mistake, you aren't meant to be with him. You're not to blame if you fell in love with someone else."

"Oh, Mom, I don't know what to do," I say with a heavy sigh.

"I know, but you will. Amelia will be fine no matter what, because she has you, and unlike you, she will always have her dad too. Equally important, you will be okay too."

"Who do you think I should be with?" I dare to ask.

She lets out a small laugh. "Sorry, sweetie. That is where my advice ends. That is not a question for me to answer."

"Grant said he doesn't think I trust men."

"I think that's a fair statement. Did this honestly not occur to you until now?"

"Not really. I mean, I always rationalized my thoughts and actions as being practical and cautious."

"Well, you are those things. Grant is a smart man, and he's always known you had some unresolved issues related to your dad."

"You think I have issues too?" I recognize my anger is misplaced.

"We all have issues. Mine involve food. Yours involve men and trying to protect yourself."

"But what if I'm missing out by being so careful all the time?"

"It's definitely a possibility."

"You've never remarried. Are you afraid to?"

"No. I've dated, but no one I got close to considering marriage with. I really loved your dad at one point. We didn't work long-term, but that in no way diminishes what we once had. At least it doesn't for me. I like my freedom, and I decided long ago I wouldn't give it up until someone came along who gave me those extraordinary feelings again."

"Makes sense. You know, Luke is pretty arrogant."

"Yes, but he's not your father. Luke listens. He may have very strong opinions, but he has always listened to yours too. He may push, but he ultimately lets you be yourself."

"True." My mind is swimming with possibilities. "I still don't know what to do."

"Do you worry Grant would cheat on you again?"

"Part of me feels like it would be foolish to think so, but I honestly don't."

"Do you believe Luke would walk away again?"

I consider my answer carefully. "No."

"So, you do have some confidence in both of them."

"I suppose I do." My answer surprises me. It's frightening to allow yourself to have faith in people who have hurt you, to give them the power to do it again.

"Maybe ask yourself a slightly different question. Who is the one you can't bear to say goodbye to?"

My heart answers immediately, but my head muffles the response.

Chapter 20

My brain is being difficult and refuses to get on board with the decision my heart was ready to make. I tell Mrs. Bianchi a condensed version of what is going on in my life. She tells me not to worry and to take as much time off as I need. My mom agrees to help with Amelia. She takes her to school Monday and doesn't bring her home until after school on Tuesday. I use the two days to sleep. It doesn't make me feel any better. On Wednesday, I take Amelia to school and decide to try a run. It only causes me to think of Luke and the look of devastation on his face when I couldn't give him the answer he was waiting for. I come home sore, my face damp from sweat and tears.

On Thursday, I attempt to get some errands done after I drop Amelia off in the morning. I dress in sweats, a hat, and sunglasses, and pray I don't run into anyone I know. In the afternoon, I view myself in the mirror. I look like I got released from the hospital and they weren't able to heal me. I call my mom to ask if she can watch Amelia for a couple of hours. I need some time with my girlfriends.

I arrive at It's a Grind, our favorite coffee shop. Vivien is at the counter, ordering her drink.

"Hello, Jessica," Vince, the owner, calls as I walk in the door. We've been meeting here for years, so I know he will start making my chai tea before he rings us up.

Vivien gives me a big hug.

"Hi, ladies!" Emily practically yells as she comes through the door.

"What? How can this be?" I hug her.

"This has to be the first time you've ever been on time." Vivien finishes my thought.

"I'm on time because I've been home since noon." Emily waves at the coffee shop owner, who is busy making our drinks. "Hi Vince."

"You're not sick are you? I can't afford to get sick right now," Vivien says.

"Not sick, cured!" Emily bounces excitedly on her heels. Vivien and I exchange a look. "As of today, I'm unemployed," she announces, plopping down in one of the comfy stuffed chairs.

"What?" There is more alarm in Vivien's voice than Emily's mood should warrant.

"I quit. The jackass told me I would have to work the next two weekends. I explained I already had plans that included a non-refundable plane ticket to visit my mom. He said if I couldn't handle my job, maybe I should start looking for something else. I told him I would do that…starting today."

"Wait a minute. Your mom lives no more than an hour from here." I shoot Emily a knowing smile.

"Yes, but he doesn't know that." Emily winks at me.

"You quit before you had another job?" Vivien is horrified.

"I'll be fine. I have some money saved up, and I'll find something better."

"I suppose this is good news then?" I try to be positive.

"Abso-fucking-lutely!" Emily gives us a wide smile.

"Well, congratulations then," I say as Vince sets our drinks on the table in front of us. I hand him enough money to cover our order. He silently nods and doesn't interrupt our conversation.

"Congratulations?" Vivien's voice is not camouflaging her concern.

"Viv, it's a good thing. I promise," Emily says.

"I know that job was awful. I just worry."

"I know you do. That's why we keep you around, to hold Jessica and me accountable. Speaking of, you look awful. What's up with you?" Emily asks.

"Gee, thanks," I say dryly. "I'm okay."

"That sounded…not convincing at all." Emily scrunches her face.

"What's going on?" Vivien asks.

I spend the next fifteen minutes filling them in on my current mess. When I'm finished, Emily is the first to speak up.

"I'm going to be honest. You deserve to be happy and get everything you want. I don't know if Luke can give that to you, but we all know Grant can't." She has not been shy about her feelings regarding Grant and his behavior.

"He's still Amelia's father. Tone it down a little." Vivien shoots her a warning look, and Emily raises her palms.

"Listen, I get it. I'm not bashing the guy. I just want us all to acknowledge that she can do better. I'm not sure if Luke is the one for her or not, but she hasn't even talked to him about her concerns yet." Emily drinks her coffee.

Vivien looks pointedly at me. "She's right. You need to talk to him."

"Why do you sound so surprised when I'm right?" Emily pretends to be offended.

"Because you usually suggest she get over things by engaging in some sort of sexual activity." Vivien laughs.

"Based on what I've heard, a round of sex with Luke may rid her of any concerns she has," Emily says.

"I knew I shouldn't have told you anything." I throw my napkin at her. I didn't share details with her, but I did tell her he was skilled.

"Wait a minute, you had dinner with Grant? Did he ever say anything about his pants?" Emily's grin is devilish.

The day I found the incriminating text messages, I decided to do one last thing before I left, in case he thought I was simply out running errands when he came home to an empty house. I took a pair of scissors and cut holes in the crotch of every pair of pants and shorts he owned. It was symbolic more than anything, but the thought of him having to go shopping the next day before being able to go to work gave me a small sense of satisfaction.

"He didn't mention it." I was disappointed when he didn't comment on my handiwork. We're quiet for a moment before erupting into laughter.

***

I arrive at work Friday morning to find an inbox full of emails and a desk piled with paperwork. Despite the assortment of duties I could keep myself occupied with, I don't get a lot done. I consider the day a success, however, because I've managed to put on jeans and mascara. My mother's words have been swimming in my head all week. I know she is right, but I'm frustrated because I'm not comfortable with either of my choices now. How could I possibly say goodbye to either of these men?

I'm busy searching online for Christmas gifts for Amelia when my phone rings. Grant's name lights up the screen. I haven't heard from him since last Friday. When he told me he wanted to give our marriage another shot, I told him I wasn't ready to make that decision and I needed time to think. I guess my time is up.

"Hello, Grant."

"Hi. I got a call from the realtor. We got an offer on the house. A good one."

"Oh." This is not what I was expecting. The house has been on the market for several months. We put a lot of money into it, and although we didn't expect to recoup all of it, we weren't willing to undersell it by too much. A week ago, I would have been thrilled by the news. Now it feels like one more ending. It's so overwhelming, I get a little choked up.

"We can say no to the offer," Grant suggests.

I try to swallow it, but a small squeak escapes my throat.

"Calm down." Grant's voice is sympathetic. "How about you and Amelia come over for dinner, and we can talk."

"Okay," I manage to creak out.

"I can cancel a few of my late appointments so we won't keep Amelia up too late."

"All right." I sniffle. I don't remember Grant ever canceling anything for me before, and I can't help that this affects me.

I leave work early to pick up Amelia. She bubbles with excitement when I tell her we're going to the old house to have dinner with her dad. I glance at her in the rearview mirror.

She's in the backseat, looking thoughtful. "I miss that house."

"It's a very nice house." I'm afraid of the answer, but I ask anyway. "What do you miss about it?"

"Catching ladybugs in the backyard. There aren't any at the new house." There isn't a hint of sadness on her pretty face.

Not the answer I was dreading. I laugh. "Let me see what I can do about getting you some ladybugs in the new backyard. Maybe I can invite them to a pool party or something."

"Ladybugs don't swim." She smiles back to let me know she's playing along.

"I suppose you're right. I don't think they make bathing suits that small."

Amelia squeals. "Nope, and they don't make beach towels that small either."

"Is there anything else you miss about the old house?" I'm a little less worried about her answer this time.

"No, I like our new home. I like the pool and my turquoise room. My room at the old house is pink. I don't like pink anymore."

"Right. What about living with only Mom?" I may be pressing my luck, but I'm ready to confront whatever thoughts are running through her head.

"I miss not seeing Dad every day, but I still get to see him a lot. And now we do more fun stuff together."

"I'm glad you and Dad get to do more fun stuff."

"I'm glad you and Dad are friends."

Her comment surprises me. "I am too."

"Madison's parents are divorced, and she says they fight a lot, and her mom says not nice things about her dad. I'm glad you don't do that."

"I'm sorry Madison has to go through that. I think you have a great dad."

"Yep. I have a great dad and mom."

She has no idea how much her words have quieted my fears. "We're here," I announce as we pull up in front of what was once our family home.

Amelia runs up to the door, and Grant opens it before she reaches it.

"Dad, can I have something to go catch ladybugs in?"

"Ladybugs hibernate in the winter. You can see, but I'm guessing they're gone for the year."

"Mom said she will try to find some for our new backyard."

"Sounds like a plan. Hey, dinner is ordered and on its way, so why don't you wash your hands and get out plates and silverware."

"We're not having that gross food Stephanie likes, are we?" Amelia plugs her nose with her fingers.

"No sushi tonight. I ordered pasta."

"Oh good, otherwise I may have to start my diet tonight."

Grant shakes his head as Amelia continues on to the kitchen. "It's crazy how quickly she goes from sounding like a kid to sounding like a teen."

"I know. She asked me the other day if she could start wearing lip gloss to school." Grant scrunches his brows at me. "Don't worry, I told her no."

"I'm not sure I'm ready for all this," Grant admits.

"Nobody is."

"Come in. Can I get you a glass of wine?"

"I'll just grab a glass of water."

As we make small talk and wait for dinner, I survey the house. It holds so many memories, good and bad. I miss those good times, but I don't feel particularly connected to this place anymore. I expected to feel more. Amelia's right; our new house is our home.

The doorbell rings, indicating our dinner is here. Grant answers the door while I help Amelia get out napkins.

Dinner is relaxed. It is the most comfortable time we have spent together in a long while. Amelia tells us about school and about how awful Aiden is. Apparently, there was an incident involving a spork and him being sent to the principal's office.

As we're laughing and enjoying our meal, I have an epiphany. We're happy. Our once painful divorce has turned into something else. Amelia is loved and joyful. Grant and I are... friends? Co-parents? I'm not sure exactly what we are, but I know what we're not.

After dinner, we clear the table and put leftovers away. Amelia heads off to the extra bedroom to watch a movie. She makes it a point to remind us that Sam has a TV in her room. We remind her we already said no to that idea.

I refill my glass of water and join Grant in the family room, where he's waiting for me.

"First let's talk about the house," Grant says as soon as I sit in the chair across from him.

"What's the offer?"

"Five thousand under asking price, but we don't have to sell it." Grant sounds cautious.

"No, I want to. That's a good offer. I say we take it."

"Okay." He stares down at his hands. "That obviously means you won't be moving back in."

"I've put a lot of thought into our conversation. I often feel like I have to do what's best for everyone else, but sometimes that means I don't do what's best for me. Us being together tonight, I realized some things."

"Go ahead." He looks at me earnestly.

"It's ideal that a child grows up with both parents in the home, but when that can't happen, it doesn't have to be awful. You're a great dad, and I know you will love Amelia no matter what happens between us."

"Of course. I wouldn't want you to come back only because you believe it's best for Amelia. You have to realize she is thriving because of us, not in spite of us."

"You're right. And I think you were correct the other night about me always trying to protect myself. It's hard for me to trust people sometimes, but I'm going to work on it."

"I'm sorry I let you down. I let myself down too." He stares at the expensive wood flooring he insisted we buy.

"I know you are, and I don't think you'd do it again." I'm instantly lighter as the words exit my mouth.

"But it's not enough, is it?"

"In a lot of ways, I still love you and always will. We had a good life together, and we made a pretty incredible little girl. I would have stayed with you forever. I would have sacrificed anything, including my own happiness, to keep our family together, but you obviously weren't happy either."

"Do you think counseling would have helped?"

"Maybe, maybe not. There were a lot of little things we did wrong that led us here. We didn't communicate. We didn't make each other a priority. We let the problems grow too big."

"And it's too late now?"

"I wish it wasn't, but for me, it is." It's a heartbreaking thing to admit, but I'm also relieved to have made a decision.

"You're in love with him, aren't you?"

There is a trace of sadness in his voice when he speaks about Luke. "I am." It's weird admitting it for the first time to Grant, but I'm not going to hold back anymore.

"I won't say I'm not disappointed, but I respect your decision. I won't try to make this any harder on you. I owe you that." He gives me a small smile.

"I don't want to pain you with the details, but I'm not so sure Luke and I are going to be together." My heart clenches.

"Why?"

"Different lives, different dreams," I say dismissively. I appreciate his attempt to care, but this has to be uncomfortable for him. I've already said enough.

"Have we not learned anything?" He looks at me, head tilted.

"I know. I need to talk to him."

By the time we finish our talk, the credits to Amelia's movie are scrolling across the screen, and she has fallen asleep. Grant convinces me to leave her there. He even offers to bring her to me tomorrow.

I call Luke and listen to the Maroon 5 song he has as his ringtone. My heart pounds with enough force to make me seriously question if this is a good idea. After several bars of music, I'm sent to voicemail.

"Hi. It's Jessica. I guess you already know that by seeing my name on your phone," I ramble. "Anyway, I need to talk to you. I don't like how things...I didn't say some things I needed to. Ugh...I would rather talk to you in person, but I would settle for a phone call."

He does not call back, and I don't sleep.

Chapter 21

*I*t's still dark as I pull into the parking lot of It's a Grind. The owner, Vince, is unlocking the doors as I exit my car. I order two large coffees, extra hot, so they will stay warm long enough for me to drink them both. The drive to San Francisco should take me about seven hours.

I make it in six.

I call Grant while I search for a place to park. I ask him if he will trade me weekends and keep Amelia for the next two days. He doesn't ask why and says it's not a problem.

I recognize the security guard at the front desk when I enter the lobby of Luke's apartment building. Apparently he remembers me as well, because he allows me access to the elevators without calling up first. I examine myself in the shiny, reflective walls. Considering I've been awake for over twenty-four hours and just spent six hours in my car, I don't look too bad. I step off the elevator and knock on his door.

My head is pounding again. This time it's due to lack of sleep and an unhealthy amount of caffeine. I knock again. Now my heart is pounding too, trying to compete with my head.

I double-check the time on my phone and see it's eleven thirty, too late for Luke to still be sleeping. He isn't here, or he's pretending not to be. To the best of my knowledge, he isn't traveling this weekend, but he's not answering his phone when I call, so I'm not positive. I could've called Aaron, but I didn't want to drag him into this. I hope I didn't waste my time coming here. I go back downstairs to see if the friendly security guard will give up any information about Luke and when he may be returning.

I press the elevator button and wait. The light blinks, indicating the elevator has arrived. I hear laughter as the doors open. I inhale sharply when I see who is inside. Luke turns his head toward me. The look of shock on his face isn't exactly welcoming. The blonde standing next to him seems as startled to see me as I am to see her.

I consider running. I'm sure there has to be a stairwell around here somewhere. But I don't. I freeze and summon every ounce of fortitude I possess. I drove a long way to talk to this man, and I need to do what I came here to do. I need to hear Luke's responses for myself, no matter how painful it may be.

He gives me a hard stare before turning to the woman. "I'm sorry, but I have to deal with her. I'll see you later tonight." His words make my stomach churn. I don't know if it hurts worse to hear him refer to me so coolly or knowing he has plans with this woman later.

"No problem, Luke." She hesitates, not eager to leave.

"I'm sorry," he says again, genuinely apologetic to be sending her away. I may vomit all over the designer wood planks. "I'll call you when I'm done." Luke steps out of the elevator.

She gives me a tight-lipped smile, not appearing the least bit threatened by me. I wish I could say the same. I'm only marginally relieved when the elevator doors close.

He walks past me and unlocks the door to his apartment. I follow him inside and notice for the first time he is in running clothes. Was the blonde wearing running clothes too? I can't remember. Everything is blurry, like a dream. My legs weaken, and I stumble but catch myself against the doorjamb. Luke turns and grabs me around the waist. The nearness of him is excruciating. I want to wrap my arms around him, but I'm afraid I'll only further embarrass myself if I do.

I don't have the energy to even pretend to protest as he walks me the rest of the way into his apartment and sits me down on his couch. He leaves, and when he comes back, he is carrying a glass of water. I drink half of the contents before setting it down on the glass coffee table.

He takes a seat at the opposite end of the large couch. "You look awful."

"Thanks," I say sarcastically.

"Are you all right?"

"I'm just exhausted. I've been up all night, driving. I obviously didn't plan this very well. You wouldn't answer my calls, and then I get here and you're with another woman—"

"Jessica—"

"You don't owe me an explanation. I'm simply stating why I look the way I do."

"I don't owe you an explanation," he says in a controlled tone and runs a hand through his hair. "I saw the look on your face when the elevator opened."

I retrieve the glass of water. I'm not particularly thirsty, but I need a distraction, however small.

"Her name is Christina." I could have gone my entire life without knowing that. "She is our new partner. She was stopping by to pick up some files to review for a business dinner we're attending tonight. She ran into me as I was finishing up my run and came up with me."

"Oh." My single-word response is quiet. I look at the glass. Instead of feeling relieved, I feel foolish for jumping to conclusions.

"Aaron and I knew when we met her we should bring her on board. She's extremely smart and a great fit for the firm." Luke crosses his arms. "So, what's so important you came all this way to see me?"

My hands are shaking. I set the glass down carefully. "Since you won't answer your phone, here I am." Luke stares at me, waiting for me to continue. I swallow. My throat feels dry despite all the water I just drank. "I didn't go back to Grant. I know it felt like I chose him, but I didn't."

"Well, you didn't choose me," Luke snaps, and I flinch.

"I didn't not choose you. I needed time to think."

"Isn't that what you've been doing this entire time…thinking? You've been trying to think your way out of a relationship with me for weeks."

"Is that what you believe I've been doing? No wonder you're angry." I shake my head. "I haven't made this easy on you—or on myself for that matter. I was trying to do the right thing, but every decision left me feeling like I was doing something wrong."

"Sounds like some issues a psychologist could help you with more than I can," Luke replies dryly. He's acting smug and cold, but I can see the hurt in his eyes.

"I'm not asking for you to fix anything for me. I want to be with you—"

"I know the 'but' is coming."

"I'm concerned about things I haven't had enough courage to talk to you about."

"I'm all ears." Luke works hard to keep his tone emotionless.

I take a big breath and release it. "I worry we don't want the same things."

"That's a pretty vague statement. You're going to have to be more specific than that." He's definitely not going to make this any easier.

"For starters, you live in San Francisco, and I live in Temecula. I know you love it here, but I can't relocate."

"I do like San Francisco. I like Temecula too. I already realized at some point I would need to move there."

"What about Aaron? Won't he have a problem with that? You have responsibilities to the business."

"I appreciate your concern, but I'm capable of sorting out my own affairs."

I remind myself that he's upset and his attitude is reflecting that. If I want this conversation to go anywhere, I need to be patient. "Of course."

"It's part of the reason we hired Christina. Aaron and I already talked about me spending more time there and traveling less." Luke tone is softening.

"You didn't tell me that."

"It was going to be a surprise." He uncrosses his arms. "I'm assuming you have additional things on you mind."

I take a deep breath. "You said you don't want kids."

"I did say that, and I also said I would make a good step-dad to Amelia someday."

"You did, and that's great. The thing is…what if I want more kids someday?"

"You never mentioned wanting more children."

"I don't know for sure, but I do know I'm not ready to close the door on that possibility."

"Didn't you tell me you didn't want more? That you're happy with one? If this is so important to you, why is this the first time we're talking about it?"

I hear his confusion. I instantly regret that I haven't been clearer with him. "I would be happy with one if that's my fate, but I would like to try for at least one more. I could have been more upfront with you, but I was trying to navigate my own feelings before I burdened you with them. Whenever the subject was brought up, you were honest about not wanting kids of your own. I didn't want to make it an issue until I knew for sure it mattered to me."

He gets up, walks to the windows, and stares out at the city for several minutes.

"You determined we're not compatible because I responded carelessly to a question I didn't realize I was being asked."

"You didn't respond incorrectly. Some people don't want kids, and that's fine. It means we want different things in life though."

"What if I change my mind?" He turns to face me.

"People don't generally change their minds about something like this. I'm sure you have reasons why fatherhood isn't appealing to you."

"Maybe I simply haven't been mature enough until now to make that kind of sacrifice."

"A child shouldn't be considered a sacrifice."

"The child isn't the sacrifice. The sacrifice is me letting go of some long-held beliefs about what kind of man I am."

"What kind of man do you think you are?" I ask, tilting my head.

He sighs. "I didn't exactly have the best role model for a father, and I realize how much like him I am. I've always thought I would be about as good a father as he was. I didn't particularly want to put another kid through the stress of having a dad like that."

"You may be like your dad in some ways, but not all. You don't have any problem expressing your love for others," I say softly.

"It wasn't easy, living up to his expectations, but I managed. I'm arrogant and driven, like he is, like he taught me to be. It works for me in a lot of areas of my life, but those aren't great qualities in a father." Luke places his hands in the pockets of his hoodie.

"Just because you didn't like how your father displayed those qualities, doesn't mean you couldn't use those same traits in a more positive way with your own kids." I'm startled by his lack of confidence.

"Maybe, but what if I can't? I don't want to have kids that can't stand to be in the same room with me." He looks at his running shoes.

"Lucas Taylor, you have excelled at almost everything you have ever attempted. Why in the world would you assume being a father would be any different?"

"Because it is different. If I fail at anything else, it ultimately doesn't matter. I mean, it does to me, but it doesn't affect anyone else. Being a parent is different. I don't want to mess up someone else's life."

"Then you don't."

"That's a very oversimplified statement."

"Not really. Sure, all parents make mistakes, but nobody really knows what they're doing. It's easier to get it right than you think. You love them and are there for them and try to do what's best, and in the end, they end up all right."

He shrugs.

"I didn't come here to convince you to want kids, but I do believe you would make a great father. You push everyone to do their best, but you do it by building them up, not tearing them down. You love fiercely and have more compassion in you than you acknowledge. I can't believe I'm saying this, but there are some things you don't give yourself enough credit for."

He sits next to me on the couch. My heart races at his decision to be near me. He looks me in the eye to make sure he has my attention.

"Having a family hasn't been a plan of mine for a very long time, but neither were you. You came back into my life and changed everything. You are a game changer for me. I've experienced how I feel when I'm with you and how I feel when I'm not. I understand what's at stake if I lose you again."

"This isn't something you can do for me." I hide my trembling hands by folding them in my lap.

Luke smiles, and I hold my breath. "The truth is, I love kids. My reluctance to be a father has been about my fear of not being a good one. It's a fear I'm ready to overcome. Besides, have you ever known me to do anything I didn't want to?"

I breathe again, and a small laugh escapes. He takes my face in his hands and wipes away the tears that have spilled down my cheeks.

"My life was missing something for a long time. Then I found the youth center, and things improved. Then I found you again, and life got even better. I'm beginning to see that having a family may be exactly what I need." He pauses and plants a small kiss on my hungry lips. "We need to promise each other something before we go any further."

"What?" I croak.

"No more leaving. We stay and we talk and maybe we even fight, but we don't leave. We are meant to be together." His bright blue eyes are shining.

"No more leaving."

When he presses his lips against mine again there is no doubt I've made the right choice. Our kiss finishes communicating everything we couldn't find the right words to say.

I awaken in a dark room. I turn on the small lamp on the nightstand and reorient myself. I'm in Luke's bed.

I pick up my phone from the nightstand to check the time. It's seven o'clock. He won't be home for a couple of hours from his business dinner. He told me I was welcome to come, but I declined. Luke left no room for me to feel threatened by Christina or any other woman. He'd told her all about me, and her advice was that he better fight for me and our relationship. I mistook her look on the elevator as one of pity because my relationship was ending. Now I realize it was a look of compassion, because she hoped it was a beginning.

He refused to make love to me earlier. He said it wasn't healthy I'd been awake so long. He practically had to pry me off him and insisted I take a nap. My adrenaline masked my exhaustion, and I didn't realize how much I needed sleep until I lay down. I don't even remember falling asleep, but I do remember Luke kissed me on the forehead and said he was leaving for his dinner and would be home by nine.

I packed a small bag, but it is still in my car, which is parked halfway down the street. Making due with whatever I can find in the apartment is a better option. I check out the guestroom and am disappointed to find nothing usable.

I return to Luke's room and search through his drawers for something to sleep in. Socks and underwear are neatly folded. A drawer of pajama pants may be an option, depending on what else I find. I move to the drawers on the opposite side of a long dresser. I'm surprised when I open the first drawer and find women's clothes. Not women's clothes, *my* clothes, the ones I used when I was here before. I take out a pair of satin pajamas.

My brands of shampoo, conditioner, and shower gel are waiting for me in the shower. While I wait for the water to heat up, I locate a towel and set it within reach. I strip off the clothes I've been wearing entirely too long and step under the hot, soothing water.

I wash my hair and am rinsing out the shampoo when I'm startled by the shower door opening.

"Didn't mean to scare you." Luke closes the door behind him.

My first impulse is to be angry with him for sneaking up on me, but when I see him looking at me like he's going to make me forget every bad moment I've ever had, my reaction changes.

"I thought your dinner went until nine."

"I decided they could finish without me. I have more important business to attend to." His beautiful mouth curls into a mischievous grin.

"Like what?" I'm breathless even though he hasn't even touched me yet.

"Turn around." I don't even consider questioning why. He leans in but still doesn't touch me. He brings his mouth close to my ear. "Close your eyes."

Just when I'm considering taking matters into my own hands, I feel the soapy bath puff glide down my back. The puff makes several trips across my back and legs. I desperately need him to touch me.

"Luke," my voice comes out in a whimper.

He doesn't respond verbally, but turns me around and washes my front. When I feel like I can't take anymore, he turns me around again and kisses the back of my neck. It is my absolute favorite place to be kissed. It sends chills through me, and I moan softly.

He reaches around and caresses my breasts with one hand. His light touch makes my nipples harden, and I moan louder, hoping he takes the cue that I want more. He reaches down between my legs with his other hand, gently rubbing until I'm panting.

"I need you," I plead.

He swiftly spins me to face him and pushes me against the shower wall. He presses against me, kissing me hard on the mouth. We grab and pull at each other, never seeming to be able to get satisfyingly close enough.

He breaks the kiss, his lips just out of reach from mine. "I love you, Jessica."

These are not merely words. They're a promise.

"I love you too."

He turns off the water and lifts me in his arms.

When I realize he's carrying me back to bed, I don't object, even though we're soaking wet.

He lays me down. "I'm going to spend the rest of my life trying to deserve you."

He is giving me something I know he has never given to anyone else, and any worries I had are erased.

I smell breakfast before I open my eyes. I jump out of the guest bed and pull on the socks I brought in here to protect my feet against the chill of the wood floors. Luke's bed was in no condition to sleep in after our shower ended abruptly last night. When I enter the family room, Luke turns around from his station at the stove and smiles.

"Good morning, beautiful."

"Good morning."

"Sleep well?"

"I did."

"Sit, and I'll get you coffee."

"You don't have to wait on me. I'll get it."

He grabs me and turns me around. "Sit," he commands. "I'm happy to get you a cup of coffee."

I sit on a barstool.

"I don't have much food in the house, so we're having eggs and grapefruit."

"That's fine with me."

"We can stop and have lunch on the way."

"I would love to spend the day with you, but I have to go home today. Grant will be dropping off Amelia this evening, and I have to go into work tomorrow."

"I figured that. I'm going to drive you home."

"That's really not necessary."

"There's absolutely no way I'm letting you drive back by yourself, so stop protesting." He places a large mug in front of me.

"Actually…" I trail off.

"What?"

"I know it's last minute, but I'm hosting dinner for my mom and friends on Thursday," I say.

"Are you inviting me to Thanksgiving?"

"Yes, unless you already have plans."

"I was supposed to go over to Aaron and Andi's, but I like your invitation better."

"Are you sure?"

"Absolutely. They'll understand. I could tell they were disappointed when I didn't already have plans with you."

"I really like them."

"Me too." He cuts open the grapefruit.

"One more thing though. I have Amelia for the entire week." I wait for him to look up at me, but his attention remains on our food.

"You said you were having friends over. I can simply be another one of your friends." He plates our eggs.

"I don't want to do that."

He finally looks at me, head cocked. "So you're saying…?"

"I want you to meet her, Luke. I mean officially, as my boyfriend. I'm positive you two will like each other." I hold my breath.

"Are you sure?" He's excited but trying to conceal it.

"I am." I'm surprised that I feel this strongly about it being time for them to meet. "You can meet her tonight if you want."

"I'm ready, but only if you are." He gives me one last opportunity to second-guess my decision, but I don't need it.

"I'm ready."

Suddenly Luke rushes around the kitchen, putting things away.

"What are you doing?"

"We need to hurry. I want to make it to Temecula as early as possible."

Chapter 22

I savor the sounds of my family and friends coming from the other room. They are playing games, talking, and enjoying each other. I float around the kitchen, checking on food, feeling more thankful than ever.

"What can I help with?" Vivien asks.

"I'm good right now. In about an hour, you can help me get everything on the table."

"I may not be able to cook, but even I can't mess that up." We laugh.

Vivien cooked dinner for Emily and me years ago. When she plated the meal, it looked fine, but the chicken was rubbery and the rice was undercooked. We only had to suffer through a few bites before Vivien silently stood, retrieved her phone, and called to have pizza delivered.

"Thanks again for having Ed and me over. When his mother came down with the flu, I thought we'd end up in a restaurant." Vivien pours herself another glass of wine.

"I'm glad you're here. I still can't get used to him wanting to be called Ed though."

"I know, but he's adamant he doesn't want to be called Eddie anymore." She rolls her eyes. "Hey, I wanted to tell you,

Luke is pretty amazing. The way he's made himself part of the group, the way he is with Amelia, the way he is with you."

I wear the wide grin I've had plastered on my face all day.

"The way you described him, I pictured him a lot different."

"Oh, he can be intense and cocky, but he's also charming and fun."

"I like him, and it's nice to see you so happy." Vivien comes over and gives me a hug.

Luke strides into the kitchen. "Am I interrupting something?"

"We were talking about you," she says. "Don't worry, it was mostly good things."

"Mostly? You're a horrible liar. If you were talking about me, it could only be good things." He smirks, grabs a green bean from the pan on the stove, and pops it in his mouth.

"See what I mean?" I raise an eyebrow at Vivien.

She smiles and shakes her head. "I better check on Eddie. I mean Ed."

Luke glances around the kitchen. "What can I help with?"

"Nothing. How's it going out there?"

"Good. Amelia beat me again at checkers." I reintroduced him to Amelia Sunday night, and over the last few days, they've become fast friends. I forewarned Grant, and even though he wasn't thrilled about it, he kept any misgivings to himself. He realizes he can't say much, considering he introduced Amelia to Stephanie. "Your mom is warming up to me. She even laughed at a few of my jokes."

"That's the wine talking."

She came over for dinner Tuesday night. Apparently, while I was putting Amelia to bed, she had a conversation with him.

She warned him not to mess things up again, or he'd have to deal with her.

"She has only forgotten how much she likes me. Once she remembers, we'll be fine."

My mom does like him, but she's going to make him work for her approval.

Luke stands behind me and massages my neck as I season the potatoes cooking on the stove. "Ed asked if we would like to join him and Vivien for dinner this weekend."

"Sure, if you want to."

"I like Ed. Seems like a nice guy. I like Rick too. Sounds like they may be joining us as well."

Rick is Emily's new boyfriend. It's the first time any of us are meeting him, but he seems like a good guy. He has a stable job, isn't covered in tattoos, and drives a car instead of a motorcycle. In other words, he's not Emily's usual type. I've caught her staring at him a few times today and can tell she's completely enamored with him.

"Sounds good. I'm glad you like them. They've become a big part of my life."

"Then they'll become a big part of my life too." He kisses me on the cheek and returns to the other room.

The oven timer rings, indicating the turkey is ready to come out. I grab my potholders and lift the heavy pan out as my mom enters the kitchen.

"Got it, hon?"

"Yeah." I set the bird on the counter.

"What do you need help with?"

"I need to get all the sides out of the lower oven and make the gravy."

"How about I tackle the gravy while you get your other dishes ready?"

I buzz around the kitchen, pulling out assorted serving dishes.

"Jessica?"

"Yeah, Mom?"

"Luke is really great with Amelia. He's been hanging out with her a lot today. That man lights up whenever she pays him any attention."

"I know. I've seen it too." It warms my heart that she's noticed.

"I will still cause him great bodily harm if he screws this up, but, I'm glad he's here. I forgot how charming he is."

The kitchen is invaded by several additional sets of hands ready to be put to work. We get dinner on the table in record time. The eight-person table seats us all perfectly. My heart swells at the sight of all my favorite people here at once.

"I would like to make a toast." Luke stands behind his chair. "I have a lot to be thankful for this year. My life is quite different than it was a year ago. It's better and I'm happy to be spending Thanksgiving with a group of people whose love for each other can be heard and felt. I'm most thankful that the woman sitting next to me has a big heart, a great family, and special friends she wants to share with me. Before we eat, I want to share a quote from Albert Schweitzer with you. 'At times, our own light goes out and is rekindled by a spark from another person. Each of us has cause to think with deep gratitude of those who have lighted the flame within us.' Thank you, Jessica, for being my spark."

I'm speechless. The whole table is quiet for a moment.

Ed breaks the silence. "Thanks a lot, man. You're making me and Rick look like real losers," he jokingly complains. Everyone laughs, even Amelia.

"Sorry, Ed. I was going for heartfelt, trying to avoid crossing over into cheesy."

"I believe you nailed it." My mom winks at him.

"Vivien's birthday is coming up. Maybe I should pay you to write her card for me." Ed laughs, and Vivien playfully punches his arm.

"I'm only inspired by two girls." Luke looks at Amelia and gives her a thumbs-up.

I haven't eaten a bite of dinner, but I'm already blissfully full.

Epilogue

The last two weeks have been dizzying. With Luke and me finally on the same page, I thought life would slow down. I couldn't have been more wrong.

It was one week after Thanksgiving when I realized my period was late. I was surprised at first until I remembered how carried away we got in Luke's apartment in San Francisco. Between the soaked sheets and the overwhelming feelings, we didn't care about ramifications. Now we have to.

It took several positive pregnancy tests and a week of building up courage for me to resolve to tell Luke. Even though he's expressed openness to having a child in the future, neither of us were planning on this so soon. I figured we would have some time to enjoy the relationship and ease into that discussion again at a later date.

Luke just flew into town this evening and looks exhausted. I consider waiting until tomorrow to tell him. He's only been here an hour, and he's already eyeing me suspiciously. I know I can't wait any longer to tell him.

We sit down to eat and I pick at my food. "Dinner is good," I say, attempting to make small talk.

"You've barely touched your fish." He raises an eyebrow.

"I'm just not very hungry, but it's good."

He sets down his fork. "I can tell you have something more important to talk about than my grilling skills. By the way you're acting, I get the feeling it's not good news. Spit it out already." He raises his voice just enough to make me wince.

"I'm pregnant." I blurt the words out instead of giving the lovely speech I had planned.

He studies me for a moment, like he didn't hear me correctly. Then his face pales.

"Are you sure?" he asks in an unsteady voice.

This is the reaction I expected, but dreaded. Tears fill my eyes.

Luke meets my eyes, and his expression changes. He blinks rapidly and shakes off whatever panic he felt. He smiles at me across the table. "Jess, are you sure?" he says, more gently this time.

I give him a small, tentative smile. "I took a few tests. I should be almost five weeks along. I know we agreed to discuss it. Having a baby this soon wasn't the plan."

"Come here." He nods to me. I walk over to him, and he pulls me into his lap. "Is this why you've been acting weird all week? I thought maybe you were having doubts again. I was gearing up to argue my case. Your announcement caught me off guard, that's all." He brushes the hair away from my face and gives me a full smile. "This is fantastic news. I hope you're happy about this."

"I am. I just wasn't sure you'd be."

"I'm sorry. I was shocked, but I can't remember ever being happier." He presses his lips to mine and proceeds to show me just how happy he is.

It's only been a week since I told Luke I'm pregnant, but things already feel different. His less-than-ideal initial reaction has been replaced by an enthusiasm I wouldn't have predicted. He changed his plans and spent the past week in Temecula with me. His excitement has made him even more appealing to me. It was downright sexy when he came home a couple nights ago with a baby name book.

We're enjoying this time when we're the only ones who know. We're waiting until after my ultrasound next week to tell Amelia, and we decided to wait until Christmas to tell everyone else. Luke asked if we should be nervous to tell Amelia, but I assured him that she will be giddy about her impending big-sister status.

This morning we ordered some baby onsies with sayings like, "If Mom and Dad say no, call Grandma." I can't wait for my mom to open them. She's going to be thrilled. I asked if we should do something similar for Luke's dad, but he said it wasn't necessary. He said he calls him every year on Christmas, so he will tell him then.

Amelia is with Grant this weekend, so Luke and I are out purchasing last-minute gifts. I told him Amelia didn't need anything else, but he insisted that he get her a gift specifically from him. He talked me into going all the way to San Diego to a specialty store he found online.

"The store's in Rancho Bernardo?" I comment as I glance up from my phone and notice we're taking a familiar exit. He doesn't answer, and I resume reading an article about photography that Luke emailed me this morning.

"Here we are," Luke says a few minutes later, turning off the car.

I'm confused when I look up. "Why are we at Rancho Bernardo High School?"

"A friend of mine from Florida emailed me and asked if I could take a few pictures of the campus. They are considering moving here, and he wanted to better view of a few things."

"Okay, I'll wait in the car." I return my attention to my phone, and Luke shuts his door.

I'm startled when he opens mine. "Come with me. It'll be fun to see the old campus."

I smile at him and put my phone in my purse. We walk the grounds and recount several memories of our time there. We round a corner, and I stop. We're at the cafeteria. There are dozens of arrangements of stargazer lilies and white twinkle lights in the trees. Maroon 5 plays over an audio system that appears to have been set up just for the occasion.

"Luke—" When I turn to look at him, he's on one knee.

"I didn't appreciate it at the time, but this is where my story changed. Years ago, in this spot, I met the most captivating girl I would ever meet. The fact that you reciprocated any of those same feelings was astonishing to me. It took us a long time to figure it out, but we finally did." He opens the small box in his hand, and I place my hand over my mouth, trying to stifle the gasp. "I'm a better version of myself when I'm with you, and I promise to never take that for granted again. I'm not simply asking you to be my wife, I'm asking you to build a life with me."

"Yes!" I throw my arms around him, and he falls backward. "Oh my gosh! Are you all right?"

"I'm better than all right." He sits on the concrete and pushes both hands into my hair. His mouth claims mine forcefully.

After several minutes, my lips are numb. I pull away and try to catch my breath. "We better stop."

"I didn't plan this part out. Now I have a long, uncomfortable car ride where I try to keep my hands off of you. I should have proposed that night in my apartment, then I could've done all the things I'm imagining doing to you." He briefly kisses me one more time and stands. He extends a hand and pulls me to my feet. "I almost did, you know?"

"Almost did what?"

"Almost proposed to you that night. I knew then I'd never make the mistake of losing you again."

"Really?" I smile. "I figured the proposal was sped up by the pregnancy."

"Nope. After I restrained myself from doing it that night, I decided to wait. I didn't want to scare you, so I told myself I had to wait at least six months. That rule was voided once you told me about the baby." He grins. "Speaking of, what do you think about the name Jackson for a boy?"

"That's my mom's maiden name."

"I know."

"I like it," I say. "Any girl names picked out?"

"I was thinking about Caroline, but we can discuss other names too. I'm sure you have some you're thinking about."

"Caroline is a beautiful name." I place my hands on his cheeks. "I think naming our daughter after your mother is a lovely idea."

He grabs one hand and kisses my palm. He holds on to it and starts walking.

"We can't just leave this all here." I glance back at the beautiful flowers.

"I have someone coming to take care of all this. I need to get you home, so I can take care of you."

My ultrasound goes smoothly. I'm as in awe as I remember being when I saw Amelia for the first time. Luke stares at the screen the entire time, mesmerized. When the doctor says everything looks perfect, Luke squeezes my hand, but his eyes never leave the black-and-white monitor.

Amelia is as thrilled about being a big sister as I knew she would be. It's all she's talked about since we took her out for ice cream and told her. She keeps asking how soon we will leave her to babysit her little brother or sister. I gently remind her she's only eight and not quite old enough to care for a baby on her own. She brightens up when I tell her I'm going to need her help from time to time feeding and changing the baby.

Christmas arrives in its usual frenzied but welcome fashion. I always run out of time to do everything on my list, and this year is no exception. I stress and worry about fitting it all in until Christmas Eve, when I let it all go and enjoy.

Amelia will spend tomorrow with Grant, so we're going to my mom's house tonight to celebrate with her. We pull into the driveway, and I tell Amelia she can head inside. She is a blur of red, her dress swishing as she bolts for the front door.

"You ready?" I ask Luke.

"You really don't think Amelia will just tell her for us?" he laughs.

"I made her promise not to. I think she likes being included in the surprise. Besides, I told her if she kept the secret until the big reveal, she could have extra dessert."

"Bribery? I like it."

"I do not bribe my daughter. I reward her for good behavior." I push Luke's arm, and he exits the car.

It takes us three trips to get all the presents into the house. We probably could have done it in two, but Luke is being overly cautious and will only allow me to carry the lightest gift bags.

"Dinner is ready." My mom calls from the kitchen. We join her, and she hugs us both warmly. "Let me see it."

I hold out my hand.

"Nice work, Luke. It's a stunning ring."

"For a stunning woman," he says as he grabs the dishes that are ready to take to the table.

Throughout dinner, Amelia wears a large grin and fidgets anxiously in her chair. I put my finger to my lips, reminding her to keep our secret when my mom isn't looking. My mom assumes Amelia is ready for presents and doesn't question her obvious excitement.

After dinner, Luke helps with dishes, and I get the dessert out. My mom has made apple pie, her specialty and my favorite.

"We can finish these later. I don't want to torture Amelia by making her wait too long to open her gifts," my mom says, setting down the dishtowel.

"Grandma, open this one first." Amelia bounces over.

"That's okay, honey. You can go first."

"I really want you to open this one first. The suspense is killing me," Amelia says.

My mom laughs. "If you insist." She tears the paper off and opens the small box. When she folds back the tissue paper, she raises a hand to her mouth. "Is this a joke?"

"I wouldn't do that to you," I say.

"I'm going to be a big sister!" Amelia jumps up.

"Oh my goodness! I'm getting another grandchild?" She has tears in her eyes.

"You are," I say.

She walks to me and embraces me tightly. "Oh, Jessica."

"I'm a little over seven weeks along."

She waves Luke to join us. "Come here." She lets go of me and grabs Luke by the shoulders. "Are you ready for this?"

"Absolutely." He beams.

My mom hugs him tightly. "You're going to be a fantastic father. We're lucky to have you join our family."

My mom finally releases him and I see his eyes are damp.

"Now everyone is crying?" Amelia sounds annoyed. "This is good news. You're all ruining my happy moment."

"They're happy tears, Amelia," I say.

"The happiest," Luke adds as he wraps his arms around me.

Thank you so much for buying this book!

To read more about Jessica and Luke's story look for

Shattered
To be released this winter

If you would like to receive updates about new releases, contests and other information from this author go to AuthorJenniferKThomas.com to sign up for her newsletter or follow her on Facebook at @authorjenkthomas.

Acknowledgments

This book wouldn't have been possible without the support, guidance and wisdom of some amazing people.

To my beta-readers, Chelle, Kathi, Lana and Vanessa. Thank you for reading early drafts and helping me tighten up Jessica's story. Your insight was helpful, but so was your encouragement.

To my editors LS and Holly. As a first time author, I can't thank you enough for all your help. I considered all your notes to be mini lessons on writing and am grateful for everything I learned.

To Fiona Jayde. Thank you for designing a beautiful cover that completely exceeded my expectations. You really went above and beyond in creating a wonderful package for my work.

To Tamara Cribley. Thank you for making the inside of my book as pretty as the outside. Your attention to detail is greatly appreciated.

To Esther at Studio Dernbach. Thank you for taking my author pictures. They turned out great and you made the experience comfortable and fun.

Thank you to all of my wonderful teachers, fellow writers and dreamers. I've learned more about writing and the publishing industry this year than I imagined and I can't wait to see where this road takes me. Thank you all for your welcome into this crazy, wonderful writing world.

Thank you to all the readers out there. I set out to write a book that I would enjoy reading and have gotten more out of the process than I thought possible. Reading a good book is an escape into a different world for a brief period of time. I feel honored you chose my book and I sincerely hope I delivered that for you.

Thank you to all my family and friends who have patiently listened to and supported my new adventure. Thank you all for coming on this journey with me. A special thanks to those who have enthusiastically encouraged me to keep going and helped me feel less crazy for following this dream. Thank you for believing in me. The support and love I've been given during this process has been such a blessing and means more to me than you can imagine. In case any of you're wondering… No! That character is not based on you. ☺

To Kaitlyn. Your creativity and sparkly-ness inspire me every day. Thank you for being such a great daughter and an endless source of joy in my life.

To Pete. My amazing husband, who doesn't ask for a lot and gives more than he realizes. Your support and the security you provide have always allowed me to be myself and try new things. When I said I was going to write a novel, you didn't even flinch. Instead you encouraged, loved and said you couldn't wait for the movie to come out. Your optimism and strength hold us together. Thanks for always being here.

To Mom and Dad. You always told me I could do anything I wanted to do. I have to admit I never really believed you, but I'm trying to now. I wish you were both still here to see what I'm going to do next. I can't wait to tell you all about it someday.

About the Author

Jennifer K. Thomas grew up being told she could accomplish anything she wanted to, but it took her some time to realize she wanted to be a writer. After spending many years exhausting the left side of her brain in the world of corporate finance, the right side of her brain was screaming for more action. After toying with ideas and characters for years, she finally worked up the courage to write her first book.

When she's not listening to the voices in her head beg to have their story told, you may find her watching *The Real Housewives*, drinking a proper cup of tea or a great glass of red wine, or eating Mexican food.

Jennifer lives in Temecula, California with her family, including the two cutest dogs in the world.

Visit Jennifer at AuthorJenniferKThomas.com.

www.ingramcontent.com/pod-product-compliance
Lightning Source LLC
Chambersburg PA
CBHW030323200626

46816CB00006BA/1903